Next Episode

Next Episode

by
B.D. Ferguson

Seraphim
EDITIONS

The publisher gratefully acknowledges the financial assistance of the Canada Council for the Arts and the Ontario Arts Council.

 **Canada Council
for the Arts** **Conseil des Arts
du Canada**

Library and Arhives Canada Cataloguing in Publication
Ferguson, B. D., 1974-, author
     Next episode / by B.D. Ferguson.

Short stories.
ISBN 978-1-927079-41-6 (paperback)

     I. Title.

PS8611.E7373N49 2016   C813'.6   C2016-904201-4

Editor: Bernadette Rule
Design and Typography: Julie McNeill, McNeill Design Arts

Published in 2016 by
Seraphim Editions
4456 Park Street
Niagara Falls, ON
Canada L2E 2P6

Printed and bound in Canada

Table of Contents

The Con

The crowd erupted into cheering applause, pierced through with enthusiastic whistles. Dylan didn't take the whistles personally, though – the same ones had sounded for every one of the five team members already on stage. Even Paolo had gotten a few.

Can't you just enjoy your first convention? Take a breath and get out there. She pasted a smile on her face and stepped onto the open stage, into a barrage of camera flashes.

She managed a wave, then made her way behind the long table, high-fiving Rachel, Jasmine and Ben almost absently, focussed on getting to Troy and his microphone.

"Go, Dylan!" someone yelled from the crowd.

She waved again as she reached Troy. He gave her a quick, fatherly hug and whispered in her ear, "You'll be great. Relax." Keeping an arm around her shoulder, he turned back to the audience. The noise tapered off as he spoke into the mic. "It's okay for me to hug her – I've known her since she was in pigtails."

The audience's chuckle was peppered with charmed "aww"s.

"To be honest," Troy went on, "I'm just glad no one can accuse me of favouritism, because I had nothing to do with this: it was you folks, and almost eighty thousand more like you, voting from around the world, who decided she should join our team permanently. And we're really thrilled you did." As the applause started up again, his arm tightened around her shoulders in a half-hug. "We had some great experiences with all our trainees, and they all did amazing work in what were – well, you saw them – sometimes challenging environments." He made a wry face, and laughter rippled through the room again.

"Who the *fuck* touched my hair?" Paolo murmured in a mocking falsetto, just loud enough for Dylan and Troy to hear.

Dylan's smile froze. In her peripheral vision Paolo lifted his phone and, when she turned slightly to frown at him, she heard its camera shutter sound. He shrugged, pointing at his phone and mouthing, "Web page."

Troy was still speaking. "Dylan's a quick learner with great instincts, and a darn bold investigator. She's definitely got what it takes to be a full, active member of the *Operation: Haunting* team, so Dylan," he turned slightly to speak directly to her, "welcome aboard. I'm glad to have you along, no matter how dark and difficult the job." He turned back to the audience and shouted, "Ladies and gentlemen, we're here at your fantastic con to officially introduce our newest operative: Dylan Powell!"

During yet more applause – *surely their hands are getting sore?* – he handed her the microphone. *Breathe.* She blinked in another round of camera flashes as Troy stepped away.

"Wow." She cleared her throat and raised the mic again. "So… apparently I can walk into an abandoned mental hospital full of paranormal activity, but talking to a crowd this big might be more than I can take."

A sympathetic laugh this time, and strangely, that made her feel better. "Okay, let's try that again. What I should've said first was: thank you. Thank you for being such amazing fans and for voting for me." She held her grin in place until the applause died down. "This has already been the most incredible experience I've ever had. Like Troy said, I've known him for years, but even if he weren't there, if *Operation: Haunting* didn't exist at all, I'd still want to do this. And I get to work with this amazing team." She swept her hand toward the tableful of people beside her. "I just can't frickin' wait!"

Everyone laughed at that, and from the far end of the table, Rachel's overly-dramatic blown kisses sent Dylan into relieved laughter, too. She turned back to the audience. "I promise I'm not going to waste that opportunity. Thank you so much."

She handed the microphone to Troy before she sat down, and he spoke over the fading applause. "All right, folks, we've got the whole team here – new, old, and me, who counts as ancient – and I know you didn't come here to listen to speeches, so let's get the Q & A started. We've got microphones set up at both of the far aisles, so come on down."

He switched off the microphone as the excited noise and movement began. Turning his back on the audience, he looked up and down the table of team members. "Okay, show time," he said quietly. "Tell the funny stories when you can. Try not to hog the mic. Give Jas time to interpret for us. No spoilers, but Rache and Paolo are going to preview next season like we talked about. Remember there are kids here, so watch your language and behave yourselves." He looked right at Paolo as he said it, but then nodded at the other end of the table. "Ben, Jas, how's the tablet working?"

Ben murmured "Should be fine" as Jasmine scribbled "test" with her stylus, and they all half-turned to see the word appear on the big screen behind them.

"Good." He took the last chair, to Dylan's left. "Wheels up, people." He turned back to the audience just as Rachel murmured her usual response: "Sir, I never got a wheel."

"We all set?" Troy was asking the audience. "Let's start over here. Yes, ma'am: what's your question?"

"Oh, my gosh," the woman said breathlessly. "Hi, I'm Michelle. And, well, first I want to say thank you all so much for being here! It's a huge thrill. Really. I'm such a fan."

"Well, thanks for having us," Troy said, as the rest of the team smiled and answered with variations on "hi" and "thanks". Jasmine gave her thank you in American Sign Language, then scribbled OUR FANS ROCK on the tablet. The crowd burst into cheers, further flustering the woman at the microphone.

"So, my question is for Troy. How do you think your Navy career prepared you for what you do now?"

To Dylan's right, Paolo grunted. "Every goddamn time," he breathed through his teeth. His crooked half-smile looked pained.

Meanwhile, Troy had laughed a little. "I get that question a lot," he said, without a trace of boredom or accusation. "I sometimes wonder, if I had a list of all my answers, whether they'd actually make any sense." He let the laughter surge and ebb before going on. "It's harder to pin down than you'd think. But I think leadership would play the biggest part. Maybe along with that, an awareness that teamwork is key, and that having a team you can trust is essential." He looked down the table at the team and waited a moment for Jasmine to catch up with her signing. "Am I right?"

Nodding heads and murmurs of agreement answered him.

"Plus he makes us keep the van really tidy," Rachel added. "Like, OCD-tidy. Shipshape, sir-yes-sir tidy."

Laughter rolled over the audience again.

"Makes it easy to find things, though," Ben put in. "That's useful."

"Maybe, but the little sailor caps are just cruel," Rachel said, to more laughter.

To Dylan's left, Troy was shaking his head, smiling. To her right, Paolo was typing on his phone, out of sight below the table. His half-smile looked pasted on.

Dylan settled back in her chair as the session went on.

Ben was asked whether the team would use any new technology next season, and his answer was typical of him: nervous at first, then gaining speed and enthusiasm as he talked about his latest gadgetry. Dylan tried to follow his explanations but was starting to lose interest when Rachel jumped in: "And do you sleep with all of them under your pillow, or do you have some sort of schedule?" Ben blushed a little but answered without a pause, "Believe me, next time we do an overnight shoot in some drafty ruined hotel, you'll want one under your pillow, too." Rachel laughed along with the audience.

Next question: "Can you give us any idea of some of the locations we'll see next season?" Making a show of looking to Troy for permission,

Rachel leaned into the microphone and said with perfect seriousness, "Disneyland, The Eiffel Tower – we'll need climbing ropes for that, Ben – and my grandma's basement. Which is maybe the scariest place we'll ever be." She managed to keep a straight face for a few moments of audience laughter, then relented. "No, but actually, pack your bags, because we're going to be doing some travelling: Chicago, Halifax, Santa Fe, Ottawa, Vermont... and those are only the ones we've confirmed. We're still waiting for the okay on a few other amazing sites."

While Rachel was speaking, Jasmine scribbled each city name followed by an exclamation mark. She added a quick, loopy sketch that had people puzzling at the big screen until she labelled it with an arrow: FINGERS CROSSED!! Rachel nodded at it. "Big time. Add some horseshoes or something."

Troy waited until the excited applause and chatter died down before saying, "Paolo, maybe you could preview some of the reports of activity in those locations."

Probably only Dylan heard Paolo stifle a sigh before he began. "Well," he said. "I don't have my notes, but from what I remember, we've got mostly the usual reports of footsteps, disembodied voices, moving furniture, quite a few regular apparitions, full-body or otherwise. You know. The usual stuff people love." More excited applause.

A woman and a teenaged boy stepped up to the audience microphone together. The boy waved at the stage, then launched into rapid sign language as the woman next to him said, "Uh, this is my son Paul. I'm just here to interpret. He has a question for Jasmine."

"Clearly," Paolo muttered. Jasmine had already leaned forward to see more closely, grinning and nodding.

"Um, first he just wanted to say thank you all for being here. He never thought you'd come to our little convention. He figured he'd have to get himself to San Diego Comic-Con if he wanted to see you." She smiled a little. "And... he wants to thank Jasmine for showing that using sign language doesn't mean he can't have a cool job, or be part of a team. Maybe even be famous."

Jasmine's proud grin softened as the boy continued to sign.

"But his real question," Paul's mother said, her eyes fixed on her son's gestures, "is whether she ever gets scared on the job, but just doesn't show it. Because of her reputation." Paul straightened his shoulders and pulled his t-shirt out in front of him, so everyone could see *Jasmine aka Fearless* spelled out in cartoon ASL gestures above the *Operation: Haunting* logo. The audience shifted and craned to see it.

"Oh my God, I want that shirt!" Rachel squealed.

Jasmine, blushing herself now, waited for the activity to die down a little before beginning to sign her answer. Troy interpreted. "Miss Fearless is saying that it's only our fantastic editing team that makes her look so... calm and collected. She says it's all..." He frowned as Paul started grinning. "I didn't catch that last part."

Grinning, Jasmine printed POST-PRODUCTION EFFECTS on her tablet. MIRACLES, she added. She winked at Paul and touched her hand lightly to her heart.

As the laughter died down, Ben startled them all by leaning into his microphone. "Don't believe her. She really is fearless." He signed the last word, a little clumsily.

Jasmine, shaking her head, circled POST-PRODUCTION and added MAGIC and a happy face.

I am part of this now, Dylan thought in amazement. These are my co-workers and we're at a fan convention. People want to hear about how we look for ghosts. How weird is this? She sat back, grinned at the audience, and soaked it all in.

Half an hour in, a fan asked what their favourite location had been. The team looked at each other for a moment, then said "Kingston," in a simultaneous chorus. They laughed as the audience broke into whistles and enthusiastic applause.

"That was an amazing experience," Rachel said as the noise died. "A crapload of work, but so worth it. I still get goosebumps thinking about it."

"It took ages to set up, but that was some of the best evidence I've ever seen," Ben agreed, his usually solemn face almost reverent.

Jasmine and Troy were nodding in agreement, but the audience member was speaking into the microphone again. "Paolo, how about you? Kingston as well?"

The team looked over in surprise. Paolo leaned slowly forward on the table, arms crossed. "No, I don't think so," he said into the new silence. "I'd probably go with the Yorkside Jail."

Dylan stiffened in her chair. Troy turned, warning in his eyes, to watch Paolo.

"Oh, yeah?" the fan asked, over a little ripple of uneasy whispers in the audience. "Why?"

"Are you kidding? It had a pretty spectacular energy," Paolo said. "Lots of bad things, horrible things, happened there for more than a century. From a historical point of view, it's an amazing place, and we were lucky to get access at all before it was demolished. Plus of course it was a landmark case for Dylan."

The audience stirred again.

Paolo looked over at her, his eyes widened innocently. "It was your birthday, right?"

Not trusting him or herself, she forced a smile. "You bet," she managed. "Not exactly the martini bar I might've preferred, but definitely memorable." The laughter from the audience had a thread of relief in it.

"Oooh, martini bar!" Rachel jumped in with enthusiasm. "On it! Note to self." She reached over and wrote on Jasmine's tablet: FIND SPOOKY BAR.

"Wrong kind of spirits," Troy said, and everyone groaned happily. "Who's next?"

As the next fan giggled into the microphone, Dylan reached up to scratch the bridge of her nose, turning slightly away from the audience and toward Paolo. From behind her hand, she muttered, "You asshole."

His eyebrows lifted momentarily in response, but he kept his gaze on his phone, below the table. His faint, sardonic smile hitched upward as the Q&A went on.

(ᛏ)

"Damn, I hate these things," Paolo exhaled as he pulled the van door shut behind him.

"I thought it was great," Dylan said defiantly, still running on adrenaline.

"It was," Rachel said. "And he knows it."

"It went really well," Troy said from the driver's seat. "Good crowd, and everyone stepped up. Thanks, guys: couldn't have done it without you."

"Aww," Ben said, which was so unlike him that everyone burst out laughing. Even Paolo snickered.

"So what now?" Rachel asked.

Jas held up her tablet and tapped her finger on FIND SPOOKY BAR. Everyone except Paolo chuckled again.

"No bar-hopping," Troy said, even though he couldn't have seen the tablet from where he was. Jas rolled her eyes, but Dylan saw Troy smile in the rearview mirror.

"Not even one little haunted martini?" Rachel asked coaxingly. "Not one little dry hauntini?"

"What would be in that, I wonder?" Ben mused.

"I didn't say you couldn't go celebrate," Troy said. "Just no bar-hopping extravaganza, please. We have an early start tomorrow. I'd suggest you stay near the hotel."

"Sir, yes, sir," Rachel murmured. "Okay: a place near the hotel. On it."

The discussion got a little loud, and lasted until Troy pulled the van into the hotel's wide sweep of a driveway. They all piled out, blinking in the bright lights overhead, as the valet took the keys.

"Right," Rachel announced in her best Troy impression. "Go do what you have to, and meet in the lobby. Wheels up in twenty minutes." She ducked his good-natured swat, stuck out her tongue at him, then turned to Dylan. "Come on, newbie, let's go get ready. It's time to welcome you in true *OpHaunt* style."

"Actually," Troy said, "Dylan has some paperwork to sign first, then she and Paolo are going to have a little chat."

"So you're saying I can't go either," Paolo said, unsurprised.

"Yeah, but you never do anything fun anyway, sunshine," Rachel said, punching him lightly on the shoulder.

Dylan was still blinking at Troy. "Paperwork? What's this about?"

"You can catch up with them later, I promise. But this has to be done. It's standard stuff, now that you're officially onboard. And Paolo has to give you some more background."

"Oh," Rachel said in surprise. She and the others turned to look at Dylan. "You haven't done that yet?"

"Apparently not," Dylan frowned, trying to read their expressions.

Jasmine signed something too quickly for Dylan to catch, and Rachel murmured, "Don't scare her."

"Well, then," Ben said, after a moment of awkward silence. "Guess we'll see you on the other side."

⌂

"Troy, what the hell?" Dylan said as they stepped off the elevator, Paolo lagging a few steps behind. "Seriously? Paperwork?"

"Sorry, hon, but yeah. Come on. We can use my room."

"I'll get the laptop," Paolo muttered and headed down the hall.

Dylan sighed as Troy swiped his card key in the reader. Behind her confusion, she felt almost childishly annoyed. This was her reward for a good day? This is what she got, after everything she'd worked for?

She let herself drop onto the couch, and after pulling a sheaf of paper from the safe, Troy joined her. He put the papers on the coffee table in front of them.

"That's the contract," Dylan said, frowning at the top page. "I signed that already."

"I know, and I appreciate your keeping it quiet until we made it official today. But if you remember, there's a mention of a non-disclosure agreement and additional training to be conducted later. This is it." He put it on the top of the pile and left his hand on it as he turned to face her.

"What you need to understand before you sign this," he said, his face more serious than she'd ever seen it, "is that it's a legally-binding document, and it has more severe consequences than probably anything you've signed before. The work contract can be broken by either party, no harm, no foul. But this document means you keep quiet about parts of our work, and that's much harder to do."

"I can keep quiet," Dylan said. "How many times did I have to bite my tongue during that Q&A today?"

"About spoilers and personality conflicts," Troy said. "Those are only a tiny part of it."

"Troy, you've known me for years. I can keep my mouth shut."

"It's more than that." Troy sighed. "It's... we're sort of famous, as you probably realized today. We work on camera, watched around the world. We do interviews, have huge online forums, a hundred thousand Twitter followers last time I checked. We all get recognized on the street. Most of our work is public knowledge, out there for anyone to find. But we need to be sure you can keep the rest of it just between us, as a team. Even if you decide to leave."

"I've wanted to be here ever since you guys started!" Dylan said, bewildered. "I'm not going anywhere, and I know how to keep work confidential."

He stared hard at her a moment longer, then nodded. "Read it first," he said. "Carefully."

Humouring him, she did. It wasn't even a full page, and was meticulous in naming the ways she couldn't share details of upcoming training or "other work-related incidents and/or experiences, to be determined as required by designated authorities of *Operation: Haunting* and its stakeholders."

She paused, frowning, and looked up at Troy. "Designated authorities… that's you, right? And the studio?"

"Mostly."

They were both startled by a knock at the door. Dylan stared at the page some more while Troy let Paolo in.

"She sign yet?" Paolo murmured.

"She's looking it over."

"Good call." The door shut. "Hey, um. Dylan?"

She looked up to find Paolo, laptop in hand, smiling at her – a genuinely understanding little smile that startled her all over again.

"I know it's a big decision," he said. "But we've all signed it, and we all think you can handle it. Plus, even though we signed, we all manage to live normal lives. Well, as normal as we can get, hanging around with this guy." He tilted his head at Troy.

Troy grinned. "Don't put that all on me. Pretty sure the spooks get some of the blame. Hey: you did well today."

"Thanks," Paolo winced. "Didn't love it."

"I know." He clapped Paolo on the shoulder, then moved back to Dylan's side. "Well? What do you think?"

She tore her eyes away from Paolo, who had moved to connect the laptop to the room's television. "I'm not sure what to think. But I'm signing." She scribbled her name on the blank.

"Okay, then," Troy said. "Witness."

"Sir, yes, sir." Paolo came over and scrawled his signature beneath Dylan's.

Troy added the date and his own initials. "That's it, kid," he said. "You're ours now." He leaned back against the sofa and rubbed his eyes.

"Welcome aboard," Paolo said, smiling again, and to Dylan's shock, he stuck out his hand. "Paolo DeSanto… though online I go by OH_Boy."

Dylan froze. "You what?"

"Yeah, it works better onscreen. You know, *Operation: Haunting* – O.H. OH_Boy."

"But… he's everywhere online. He's –"

"Sweet?" Troy suggested. "Enthusiastic? Our biggest fanboy ever?"

Paolo scowled. "Shut up."

"No," Dylan stammered. "No way. OH_Boy is always so... happy. He's – but you're –"

"An asshole?" Paolo said.

"Yeah, let's go with that." She blinked, remembering how often the team had laughed at OH_Boy's comments and sent him smiling emojis in return. He was the most avid follower on all the online feeds.

Paolo's sardonic smile returned, resignation in every line. "Why else would you bring an archivist into the field? Think about it. Paolo plays better for the cameras."

"He's especially grumpy when we aren't finding much evidence," Troy pointed out.

"Cynical time fill: that's me." Paolo shrugged. "At least online as OH_Boy, I can say what I'm thinking. And keep the troll activity on the forums to a minimum while I'm at it."

Dylan blinked at him again, considering a variety of responses. "Huh."

"Okay," Troy said, sounding tired. "I'll leave you to it. I'm going to check in at home before it gets too late to call. If you need me, I'm just in there." He nodded toward the bedroom off the sitting area.

"What's this now?" Dylan asked, suddenly wary.

"This is the other training the contract mentioned," Troy soothed. "It's just – well, Paolo will walk you through it. If you need to, though, you can come talk to me afterwards, okay?"

"That's ominous," Dylan told him, trying a laugh. "What is all this?"

"The reason for the confidentiality clause," Paolo said.

"That doesn't help," Dylan said.

The door shut behind Troy. Paolo leaned over and switched off the table lamp. The laptop and television screens washed the room in silver-blue.

"Oh good, mood lighting," Dylan muttered, moving carefully to one end of the couch. Paolo didn't seem to notice, cuing up a video clip. He let a few seconds play before pausing it.

"Do you recognize that?" he asked, nodding at the television screen. "It was one of our cases in season two."

It took a moment for memory to shoulder past the oddness of the situation. "Isn't that the West Point Lighthouse?"

"I knew you were a superfan," he said with satisfaction. "You used to come to these cons in costume, didn't you? Admit it." He pressed play. "This is Ben, going solo with that y-spectrum camera we tried for a while."

Onscreen, an oddly-shaped room swept past in a hundred smoky shades, empty except for a staircase climbing up a far wall as if it were penciled in. Ben's calm voice echoed as he noted the time, location and equipment for his clip-on voice recorder.

"I remember this," Dylan said. "That y-spectrum made everything look really weird, but there should be… there it is." She pointed at a wisp of black shadow, blurring past the corner of the stairs as if rushing up the spiral. Paolo paused the playback again, and she couldn't help but grin. "I remember this episode. Ben was pretty shocked when he did the evidence review."

"Some of his best acting that season," Paolo said, with a return of the personality she was used to. "The review segment isn't on here – this is the raw footage. Keep watching."

"Time note, 1:12 a.m.," Ben's whisper came through the speakers. "Pretty sure I just saw something go up those stairs. Hello?" He called out as he moved closer to the stairway, tilting the camera up and adjusting the focus. "Is there anyone here with me?" Onscreen, the greyscape blurred, resolved and blurred again as he adjusted the camera settings while climbing the first few steps. His boots clanged to a halt on the metal stairs as he lifted the camera's view upward.

A tall, slender silhouette in charcoal stood about four steps above, looking down at him. The camera whirred and blurred again, trying in vain to bring its subject into focus. The silhouette's smudgy head tilted as if curious.

"Oh," Ben said. "Hello. Can you see me?"

The silhouette straightened its head and took a noiseless step down. Ben inhaled, but his voice stayed calm. "I'm not here to hurt you," he said.

A thin sound, faint but persistent, whispered through the speakers.

"I'm here with others," Ben said. "If you have a message, we can listen. My instruments will record you if you speak to me." As he spoke, the other sound grew in strength like a rising river.

Again Dylan's memory checked in. "This noise," she said slowly. "Wasn't it Jasmine's evidence for this episode? On the playback it seemed almost like words..."

"It wasn't Jasmine's originally." Paolo adjusted the sound levels and suddenly she heard, as clearly as if it had been spoken in her ear: ...*you here? You can't be here. It isn't safe. Why are you here? You can't be here. It isn't safe. Why are you here? You can't be here. It isn't safe. Why are you here? You can't be here...*

"Do you have a message for anyone?" Now Ben's voice was overloud, oblivious to the rush of whispers his equipment was recording.

Onscreen, the storm clouds churning within the figure became agitated as the voice rose in distress. *You can't be here! It isn't safe!*

It rushed the camera, turning the screen abruptly black.

Dylan jerked back in her seat as Ben cried out in alarm. The screen returned to confused life over a chaotic clatter of echoing metal, followed by a heavy impact and a pained curse. The camera hit the floor, bounced once and slid to rest with its lens facing the quiet, breezy night outside the lighthouse's front door.

"Fell backwards down six steps," Paolo said as he stopped the playback. "Bunch of wicked bruises and a badly sprained ankle. He spent a lot of that trip in the van. It took some creative editing to make it seem as if he went out a few times."

Dylan stared at Paolo as he called up another file. "Okay." Her voice sounded a little unsure. She tried again. "Okay. So – creative editing. That happens in reality television, right? Creative editing?"

"Not really the point of that clip," Paolo said dryly. He sat back, squinting at her in the low light. "That's your reaction, though, isn't it? You aren't surprised at all by the apparition itself."

"Well, sure – I mean, he actually captured something on tape, and it's pretty damn amazing. I'm sorry he got hurt, but why didn't we broadcast that piece? That's huge evidence."

"Evidence," he repeated, still studying her. Then he shook his head once. "It would've freaked out our client for sure, and at least half the audience."

"But it's incredible: sound, image, everything!"

"You do realize most of our viewers aren't fully convinced that ghosts even exist."

That made her pause. "No. That can't be right. Why would they watch, if they didn't believe?"

"To see us fail. To watch us debunk the claims. To explain away what we can't. To love Rachel and hate me. They're more interested in us than the paranormal."

"Well," she frowned, "something like this would open their eyes."

"And what a pleasant awakening it would be."

"Come on. I don't think it meant to hurt him. If he'd been able to hear the voice, he could've prepared. He might not have fallen."

Paolo snorted and turned back to the computer. "That's pretty much what Ben said himself, afterwards. Doesn't matter. He was overruled."

"By the studio? Or by Troy?"

He kept scrolling through the file list. "We're going to jump ahead, since the existence of actual spirits seems to be something you accept so easily."

"Doesn't everyone on the team?"

"Not at first," he said absently. "So we'll skip Rachel playing hide and seek with what seems like a little girl around an open grave in Chicago. Although that kid's laugh is the creepiest thing I've ever heard, before or since."

"So this is the training? Dusting off the archive footage to show me what the audience never sees?"

In the flickering light from the screens, Paolo gave her a sideways glance. "Don't make my job sound so lame." He hesitated over a file, cued it up and nodded at the television again. "Recognize it?"

"Show me more than one frame and I'll see what I can do." She sat back, torn between amusement and anticipation.

The picture shifted into motion as the camera panned across a comfortable family room with a long sofa against one wall, facing an oversized fireplace. A pair of rocking chairs waited at either ends of a pale area rug, and a low coffee table was centered within reach of everything. Rachel's voice from behind the camera was soft, but brimming with its usual cheer: "Rachel and Jasmine, Mortimer house, 2:43 am. We're going to hang out in the living room and see what happens. Voice recorders are running, Jas has the EMF, and we've set up the threshold laser just outside the room in case anything decides to join us."

"Mortimer house," Dylan echoed, shaking her head.

"Yeah, trick question. This was never broadcast. No one's seen it but us."

Onscreen, Rachel's camera was still sweeping the room. "Jas, anything yet?"

Jasmine appeared in frame, holding the electromagnetic field sensor out in front of her and frowning at its display. "Just the usual," she said, her voice as soft as Rachel's but richer, with the vaguest hint of an accent. "A few spikes near the TV and stereo, but nothing unexpected."

"Oh my God," Dylan breathed. "This... this is before she got sick. They never show these episodes anymore. Sometimes the Europe ones, but not the others."

"She had a nice voice." With a few clicks on the keyboard, Paolo moved the video ahead. "They decide to split up. Rachel leaves a camera on the mantel, and takes another with her to the second-floor hallway. Jas stays here with the EMF. I'll show you their footage simultaneously."

Rachel was sitting cross-legged with her camera set a few feet away, the hallway walls serving as a natural frame. "My name's Rachel," she said. "Can anyone hear me?"

The living room shot was a little off-center, but it clearly showed Jasmine making herself comfortable on the couch, looking around the room. "Is there anyone here with me?" she asked. "I'd like to hear your story. The family who lives here is concerned." She looked down at the EMF sensor on the table in front of her. "Do you know this isn't your house anymore?"

"The kids in this house say they see a little boy," Rachel was saying. "Is that you?"

"I'm not here to hurt you," Jasmine said.

"Can you come play with me?" Rachel asked. A high giggle, suddenly cut off, made her look around with a smile. "Hello? Was that you laughing?"

Jasmine glanced off-screen as the threshold sensor squealed, and then she noticed the EMF lights, flickering in rapid sequence. "Whoa," she murmured. "Something's here, anyway."

Rachel's voice turned coaxing. "Why don't you come play with me? I have some toys here..." The giggle sounded again.

With a gasp, Jasmine sat up on the couch, rigid. Her hands clawed up to her throat, her mouth opening and closing without a sound. In the next instant, she was thrust back against the sofa cushions, her legs pushing feebly at the table in front of her. There was the merest scrape as the table moved, and her clothes rasped against the upholstery, but otherwise her struggle made no sound. Her mouth gaped wider, her eyes flaring open, then squeezing shut.

"It sounds like you're having fun," Rachel said to the hallway, pouting. "Can't I play, too?"

Downstairs, Jasmine's hands were scrabbling at her throat as if trying to latch onto whatever had hold of her. Her body bowed suddenly up and outwards in a taut arc, throwing her head over the back of the sofa and pushing her toes into the carpet. Her muffled gasps came faster, more frantically. The sensor on the table was flickering and bouncing, spinning across the slick surface.

"I might have some candy in my pocket," Rachel said, rustling a wrapper.

A wet, crackling crunch broke the silence in the living room. At the same instant, Jasmine was yanked up off the sofa to dangle limply in midair for a moment before being thrown out of frame. She landed in a boneless tumble that set a rocking chair into motion.

Rachel frowned, looking offscreen. "Jas? Did you hear that?"

Jasmine's pained wheezing filled the living room audio. The EMF sensor lifted off the table and streaked toward the camera, striking the wall above with a sharp crack and a shower of electronic pieces.

Rachel scrambled up in alarm as heavy, running footsteps overlaid Jasmine's feeble noises downstairs. "Jasmine!" a stricken voice cried as the threshold sensor beeped. Someone raced past the camera, slowing at the edge of frame. "Oh my God… Jasmine?"

"Who… is that?" Dylan managed, her throat dry.

"Ben, of course," Paolo said as Rachel darted down the upstairs hall, the camera left behind. He closed her video, and the living room filled the screen.

Nothing was moving within the camera's view, but Ben's urgent off-screen whispering came through. "Hold on… Oh God, Jas, can you breathe? Breathe for me, come on…"

More running footsteps neared, and the threshold sensor went off again as Troy's voice filled the channel and his bulk crossed in front of the camera. "What happened? Is she all right?"

"No," Ben's voice cracked. "It's bad. We have to –"

"Troy!" Rachel shouted in the distance as one of the rocking chairs flew across the screen. Troy threw up an arm to block it, but it crashed into him hard enough to stagger him backwards into Ben and Jasmine.

"Stop it!" Rachel yelled, still offscreen but closer now. "You have no right to be here!"

A lamp somersaulted off the end table with a contemptuous crash.

"Tantrums now?" Rachel said, her voice tight with anger. "I don't think so. Stop it and get out. You aren't welcome here."

Troy rose into view, wiping blood off his forehead. "Damn straight you aren't welcome here," he said grimly. "Get out or we get you out."

The sofa cushions shuddered and split open, fabric ripping like a cursed response. Stuffing flew.

"Wow, a poltergeist pillow fight?" Rachel sneered. "Now I'm scared."

The second rocking chair raced toward her as the coffee table started jittering, two legs lifting off the floor.

"Stop *provoking it!*" Ben screamed.

"We're on it," Troy said, sharp but calm. "Get Jasmine out."

Dylan hardly knew where to look or listen as all the furniture shook violently and a gale wind spun through the room, howling past the camera's microphone. The room itself seemed to shudder as the camera rocked. Both Troy and Rachel started shouting, and it took Dylan a moment to realize it wasn't English. *Is that Latin?* She hardly had time to wonder before Ben's voice caught her attention.

"Come on, Jas," Ben whispered hoarsely. "Come on, baby, let's get you out. Hang on to me, okay?" They appeared in the corner of the screen, his arms cradling Jasmine's body as if she weighed nothing, her head lolling against his chest. He darted through the camera's view as Troy and Rachel called into the chaos around them.

Paolo stopped the playback, and the sudden silence in the room seemed to echo. "It crushed her throat so severely they were considering tracheotomy. She was lucky, but the doctors couldn't repair her voice-box," he said when Dylan didn't immediately speak.

"Wh-what happened? What was that?"

His eyes were pained, even in the low light of the screens. "Exactly what it looked like. More demon than spirit, we figure. Had to exorcise the damn thing."

Exorcise? She tried to fit that in her head. "But... how?"

"Troy was a Navy chaplain, and I guess you could say he's kept up with it. Spooky stuff runs in Rachel's family, and her degree is in comparative religions, so she's useful in a pinch. Ben... he's usually calmer in a crisis. Don't judge him by this."

Still processing, she remembered the anguish on Ben's face as he crossed the room. "Ben and Jasmine?"

Paolo sighed. "They'd kept it quiet, but when he wouldn't leave her hospital room we all pretty much clued in."

"Is it still going on?"

"Guess so. They've been engaged for about six months. The studio won't let them say anything publicly, for some useless corporate reason."

She blinked at him, the revelation looking for somewhere to settle after what she'd just seen.

He smirked a little and shrugged. "Archivist. It's amazing what I know." He went back to the laptop files as she tried to pull herself together.

"Okay," she said. "Okay. So the jobs aren't always fun. These things are real and they can be dangerous. I get it."

"And that's what you're going to go with? That's the moral of the story?"

"What else am I supposed to get out of it?"

"You could notice how we worked as a team there. If Ben hadn't been watching the monitors in the van, if he and Troy and Rachel hadn't been there to step in…"

"Right, true. And where were you during all that?"

"Or you could ask if you should pick up some Latin along with the ASL, so you can be a useful addition to our team."

"Should I? Do I have to?"

"Or," he said, "you could watch this."

Her irritated response stuck in her throat when she saw the screen. "That's… that's the Yorkside Jail."

"I know. Your birthday and your… what was it, fifth time out with us?"

"You should know," she said through her teeth, "archivist." Her heart seemed to catch as she watched familiar figures race around in fast-forward, setting up equipment. "Hey look, there's you being an ass. Oh, there it is again."

"Funny. But now you know I had to keep that up for the camera."

"So you say."

"And I couldn't show favouritism for any one trainee while the voting was still happening, no matter who I wanted to win."

She shot him a glance while he spooled through the footage. A click stopped the mad rush, and the screen filled with an odd rainbow of colours. Two figures, outlined in crimson and splotched all over with white, orange and gold, stood alone in a space made of blues and violets.

"This is from the thermal camera," she said.

"Well done."

She stared some more. "That's me. With Troy."

He nodded. "In the cafeteria, around 3am. We'd already set up the night vision camera at the end of the room. That's what gave us the footage we put together for the broadcast."

"Wait, but… that's you filming, with the thermal. You were with us." He nodded, eyes still on the screen, and irritation rolled through her again. "You told us the thermal wasn't working that night. I watched you film a segment about how its power levels had drained because the place was so active."

"Sometimes I have to lie. Sometimes we all do." His eyes met hers, but only for an instant, and in the low light of the screens she couldn't tell whether he was annoyed or ashamed. "Jasmine was never sick, the thermal worked perfectly, Troy and the team know the truth, trainees and audience don't. Have you not figured that out yet?"

She bit back a retort, her heart thumping now. "So you're going to show me something that happened that night. Beyond what I know happened that night."

He pressed play, and the rainbow figures onscreen came to life.

(th)

Dylan let herself into her hotel room, tossed her card key on the table, and headed for the window, using the glowing lights of the city below to navigate between the furniture. She stopped at the glass, crossing her arms over her stomach and leaning her forehead against the cool pane. She exhaled, and her breath condensed on the window a moment before fading away. Breathing in and out again, she watched the evidence appear and disappear.

"That," she murmured, "was a very odd day."

She tried to think back, to recapture the excitement of the fan Q & A session, but found it as distant and unreal as yesterday's dream. Shaking her head against the window, she reached again for detail, aware of the silent darkness of the room around her and a chill across her shoulders.

Remember Paul, she thought. With that came a sudden flash of clarity: a black t-shirt with cartoon hands, the sound of Rachel's enthusiastic squeal. A remembered sense of happiness rose, warming her, making her smile.

"Remember that," she told herself aloud, "not –" A vision of Jasmine, suspended gasping above a coffee table, punctured her mood. Shuddering, she shoved it away again. "Not that."

Who the fuck *touched my hair?* Paolo's mocking whisper from the Q & A darted through her mind. Her scalp prickled at the memory of fiery figures on a television screen.

"Stop," she murmured.

Relentless, the memory played on: the thermal versions of her and Troy sitting in the vast, frozen-indigo dining hall of the Yorkside Jail, talking to the air.

"Is there anyone here who'd like to speak with us?" Troy asked, his heat signature rippling as he moved in his seat. "We aren't here to hurt you."

"My name's Dylan," her own voice said, sounding strange and hollow from the television speakers. "We're here to listen to your story."

Dylan? came a soft whisper, and, nearer the microphone, Paolo drew in a startled breath. *I knew a Dylan once. Long ago. But... you're not like him.*

Two shining faces turned toward the camera, orange and gold swirling over their features. "Paolo? You hear something?" Troy asked.

"Maybe a whisper," Paolo murmured. "I think it was responding to her." The camera jerked toward Dylan, whose heat signature flared briefly.

"Me?" she squeaked, then recovered. "Hello?" she called. "If you're here with us, I'd like to meet you."

Troy held a glowing arm in the air, a box of shadows in his fist. "We have a device here that will tell us if you come closer. And Dylan has a voice recorder, so we can hear you."

A spot of steel-blue behind Dylan's chair swirled and grew, drifting up to the level of her head and hovering there as if uncertain, while Troy said "If you're here, come closer" and Paolo, hardly breathing, said nothing.

Both Troy and Dylan leaned forward to watch the K2 in his hand – and it had stayed unlit and lifeless, Dylan remembered. The sensor hadn't registered anything, and her own recorder had captured only the familiar voices of the team. She remembered the depths of the shadows, the feeling of cavernous space around them, the lingering scents of old cooking grease and body odour, the flaking paint and twisted remnants of furniture in the corners, but the sensors hadn't responded at all.

In the thermal view, the cool spot behind Dylan swirled again, elongating until it nearly touched the floor. Then it curled slowly up and toward her head and shoulders.

"Paolo?" Troy called quietly. "Anything new?"

"No," Paolo answered, after a barely noticeable hesitation. "I think... something's off with this thermal."

Sometimes I have to lie, sometimes we all do. Was she imagining a note of regret as she remembered Paolo saying that?

Onscreen in the Yorkside Jail, Troy was looking toward the camera. "Off? Like a malfunction?"

The frond of purple cold was still unfurling behind Dylan. *What are you doing here?* the voice murmured from the speakers. *This place isn't for you.* Hesitantly, the wisp of colour reached out and stroked the crown of her head.

Dylan stood up so quickly her chair fell over backwards with a clatter that echoed through the dining hall. "Someone just touched me. Touched my hair." Her heat signature flared wildly as she spun around. The room was so dark, she remembered, she couldn't see three feet past the filming area. Her voice climbed embarrassingly high, cracking. "I know I felt something. Who the *fuck* touched my hair?"

The bruise-coloured form pulled itself once more into a hovering ball. *I'm sorry, I'm so sorry. I would never hurt you.*

Troy was trying to calm her down, still asking questions to the vast dark around them. Paolo was silent, watching in the thermal spectrum as the whispering shadow rippled, swirled and flattened, finally haloing Dylan's head and shoulders without touching her. *Hush girl, don't be angry, but this place isn't for you. This place is full, too full of emptiness. It will drown you. Dylan. Dylan, you can't stay, they're coming...*

In the corners of the room, new dark clouds were coalescing, spinning and growing, drawing closer as if in curiosity. Spots of blood red and black bloomed within them.

Dylan remembered her panic rising, stronger than she'd ever felt, and how the room seemed to constrict around her. "Something's wrong. We have to leave." Her voice had been thin and brittle through the speakers, not sounding like her at all.

"Dylan, it's okay —" That was Troy.

"No! No!" She'd fought for breath, fought for control. "Something's wrong. We aren't alone here. We have to get out!"

In the playback, Paolo swallowed hard, the sound lost behind Troy's soothing noises. The smear of colour cowled around her faded into almost nothing as the bloody dark suns in the corners bobbed and grew. "Maybe we should get her out," Paolo finally suggested.

Dylan's breath heaved in and out as she looked around wildly. "I want to go back to the van. We can't stay here anymore."

"Okay, okay. We're going." Troy put an arm over her shoulders, turning for a moment toward Paolo. "What's the situation with the thermal?"

"Nothing," Paolo answered tightly. "Not a damned thing."

"Liar," Dylan whispered, blinking in her silent hotel room. Sometime during her trip down memory lane – a confusing landscape of real life and video evidence – she'd sat on the edge of the nearest bed, facing the city below.

Hush, girl, don't be angry…

"I'm not," she said, taking a deep breath. "Well, okay, I'm angry at Paolo. He's such an ass."

Except then she remembered his face just minutes ago, drawn and worried in the light of the screens as he stopped the playback and looked at her. "You have to be careful, Dylan," he'd said. "It seemed drawn to you, drawn to your energy." Hesitantly, he'd reached over and touched her hand. His fingers made the merest contact before he pulled away, turned back to the laptop, and started closing down files and programs at lightning speed. "Just be careful."

A sudden chill across her neck made her shiver. *Wasn't he just doing his job? Everyone has a role. Troy is the leader, Rachel is the comic relief, Ben is the engineer…*

"And Jasmine?" She suppressed a different type of shudder. "Guess she was the sacrificial lamb."

But she survived and is thriving. She is the courage.

She sighed. "Guess that leaves me as either Toto or a flying monkey."

A faint laugh drifted past her ear, and a lightly frosted feather seemed to brush her hand. *Never.*

"You're right. I was definitely the Cowardly Lion for that episode." She looked up into the darkness of the room. "So… the night we met, in the Yorkside Jail. You were seen."

So it seems. Amusement and irritation slid into regret. *I truly didn't mean to scare you, only warn you.*

"I know. Though now I know what you look like, at least."

That isn't what I look like. Amusement melted into uncertainty. *Is it? I don't think so…*

"Doesn't matter," Dylan said soothingly. "But we'll have to be more careful when the thermal's on." She felt the sense of rueful agreement in the air. "More importantly, you got me out of there. Thank you for that.

And now I know something about what might have happened if you hadn't."

I will keep you safe, Dylan.

"You have so far." She dredged up a smile as more of the convention Q & A surfaced in her memory. "Did you hear Troy tell everyone I have good instincts?"

The laugh sounded again, rippling goosebumps across her skin. *Yes.*

"You know that's probably the only credit you're ever going to get," she said.

I can live with that. Something tugged playfully at the ends of her hair.

So to speak.

Season Premiere

No one had told her that the catacombs beneath the old church wound on and on, deep into the dark. She'd been walking forever, breathing in the strangely comforting scents of dry dirt and ancient stone, listening to the soft scuff of her steps, calling out EMF readings.

"Zero point two. No change."

Why she was even taking electromagnetic readings down here, far below an old church that had never even been wired for the internet, was a mystery she was feeling increasingly silly about. If Troy hadn't been so adamant – "Just keep going, and keep us updated the whole time, okay? Keep giving us readings" – she would've stopped long ago. She wasn't getting anything beyond a point-two in any case and hardly even needed to check the readout anymore.

She looked up, seeing more of the same shadow-draped, rough-hewn hallway around the pale beam of her headlamp, and stopped walking for a moment to listen. Fine dirt drifted around her feet. Darkness and stillness around her, nothing more, and when she checked her watch she discovered she'd been down here for hours.

Just keep giving readings, she told herself as a faint worry rose in her. "Still nothing," she whispered, her eyes barely dipping toward the readout. "Point two steady."

She looked around for the camera team, ready to exchange a resigned smile in a *here we are again* moment of camaraderie, but found she was alone in the hallway. She turned in a circle, as if they had somehow gotten behind her. Then she remembered: Troy had told the crew to stay behind. She'd gone in alone.

But she frowned as she began to walk again, because there was something important to remember about going in alone. It slid around the edge of consciousness, slipping away when she reached for it. It fluttered at the edge of vision, disappeared into cracks and crevices when she turned to look, when her lamp chased it into the stones.

Just keep giving readings. "Point two steady."

Trudging on, she wondered why these were even called catacombs, when there were no bodies in them. The few curled and leathery corpses the church had sheltered for centuries were long behind her. She hadn't seen anyone, dead or alive, all this time. Just miles and miles of this same dry, narrow passageway, the same smells of undisturbed dust and stone, the same shadows squeezing the brightness from her light.

Then the nearby sound of a happy crowd reached her, and she smiled. Finally. She was almost out, almost to the party. She'd have to change, because she was still in her work clothes and they smelled like the underground, but at least – at last – she could put her equipment down.

One more reading, just to be sure. She dragged her eyes down, already speaking: "Zero point…" But the EMF readout had disappeared, and she blinked, blinked, blinked at it until the screen showed her a number. "Three hundred and eight," she said aloud.

She looked up and saw she was standing in a darkened house, her head lamp having disappeared unnoticed. The dim streetlight through the window blinds was just enough to discern a comfortable family room, with a long sofa against one wall, fireplace along the other, a pair of rocking chairs bracketing an area rug, a central coffee table. The rug glowed faintly, like a mushroom cap in a midnight forest, but the shadows in the corners were so thick they seemed solid.

"Three hundred and eight," she whispered, staring at the fireplace. Its waiting blackness beckoned and repelled her, and she stood, torn, in the middle of the room. Cold air sighed past her arm, and she turned to see one of the rocking chairs nodding back and forth. Instead of the creak of rocker on wood, though, another burst of party noise reached her ears. She thought she heard Troy's voice.

"Guys?" she called, rooted in the middle of the room. "Can I come? Where are you?"

The noise of the party increased, with a burst of music as if someone had nudged a stereo on and off again. Rachel shrieked something about candy, her laughter piercing the dark.

Both rocking chairs were in motion now, silent but moving steadily toward her with every forward pitch. She tried to keep them in view and still watch the fireplace. The fireplace was wrong, she knew, and needed watching. She was breathing harder, tension clenching her body, and she knew she should call for help. Troy always told them to trust their instincts and call for help when they needed it.

Staring at the fireplace until her eyes watered, she forced the words out. They emerged as whispers, barely audible. "Help. Help. Guys? I need... help..." Her voice faded further as she spoke. She opened her mouth as wide as she could, pushed all her energy into her vocal cords as a rocking chair nudged her fingers. But her voice was gone, lost to the darkness of the room. She strained until her face hurt, but not a single sound emerged.

The rocking chairs were crowded against her now, slamming into shins and elbows, while the sooty mouth of the fireplace reared up the wall and lunged across the floor toward her feet, howling as it came.

Upstairs, the noise of the party returned. She could hear footsteps and the familiar voices of her friends.

The cold black pit of the fireplace swallowed up her body as she screamed and screamed and screamed in frenzied silence –

Her mouth was wide open as she woke, her throat working itself into pain. Only the ugliest of sounds emerged, though, a thin rasp and almost animal-like mewl. She blinked sweat and tears out of her eyes and realized someone was clutching her arm in the dark. She struggled in panic a moment before his voice registered.

"Jas! Jasmine, it's okay. It's okay. It's me. You're okay."

Ben.

His voice helped to orient her, and she reached for his hand as an anchor. He never hurried her, which she appreciated. He just sat next to her, clutching her hand as tightly as she did his, stroking her hair back from her face, brushing saltwater off her cheek. He always seemed to know when it was safe to talk.

"Again?" he asked softly.

She nodded, then grimaced and wobbled her hand back and forth. This one had been a little different. Maybe her subconscious had finally revolted, just too bored after nearly a hundred nights of the same nightmare. She hauled in another breath. Catacombs: where had that come from? They hadn't been near any catacombs since the Europe special two seasons ago.

Feeling her heartbeat return to normal, she sighed as Ben gathered her close. They leaned back against the headboard, curled together with their knees drawn up as if in defence. His fingers absently drew circles on her shoulder, and this too helped her refocus. She rested her head against him, and when he spoke, she felt the sound rumble through his torso.

"It's been a few days since the last one. I was wondering if maybe they'd just stopped." He must've felt her small snort of *yeah, right,* because he moved to gently kiss her hair. "Wishful thinking, I guess. You want to talk about it?" He said it without even wondering if he should change the verb, and she appreciated that even more. Still, she hesitated.

He reached for the bedside lamp, but suddenly she couldn't bear the thought of turning on the lights just to tell the story of yet another damned nightmare. Shaking her head, she caught hold of his arm, pulled it back to his side, and returned her head to his shoulder.

"Okay," Ben said quietly. "We can talk about it later."

Great. She made a non-committal noise. She stared at her fingers as they lay on his chest and wondered if glow-in-the-dark gloves would help: then she could sign without turning on the light. It would only look a little ridiculous, she thought. It would lend an appropriately spooky, disembodied tone to the workings of her nocturnal mind. And it must be pretty late at night, she realized, to be even entertaining the idea. She glanced over at the alarm clock and winced. Moving into Ben's sightline, she gestured at the clock and grimaced again. *Sorry*, she mouthed.

"Don't worry about it."

He meant it, but she still frowned at him. They both knew he had a busy day ahead. She started, gently but firmly, to push him back down on his pillow.

"Hey," he said, capturing her hand on his chest. "I said don't worry about it." Even in the darkened room, she could see his eyes searching her face the way they searched for glitches in the equipment: alert, assessing, ready to fix anything broken.

She smiled a little at his concern, and his expression lightened. He smoothed her hair back again. "You all right?"

She nodded once, and leaned forward to meet his mouth with hers. He pulled back after a moment, running a thumb across her jaw. "You sure you're okay?"

She nodded once more before settling into his arms.

Sure. Nothing broken here.

⌘

Ben was gone when Jasmine woke again, but the smell of shampoo from the bathroom and coffee from the kitchen told her he hadn't been gone long. He might even still be in the front room –

She rolled to look over at his side of the bed and smiled. No, he was gone, but he'd left his usual sort of good-bye note: little snips of electrical wiring, wrapped in various colours with their frayed, coppery ends bright in the morning light. They were crossed in pairs, a row of small x's glinting across his pillow.

Three kisses this morning, which meant he was worried about her.

It wasn't until she was showered, dressed and caffeinated that Jasmine felt the dream finally start to recede, its impact fading as if bleaching in the daylight. She sat directly in the sunbeam, vaguely feeling that it might help, as she scrolled through the various *Operation: Haunting* fan sites on her tablet.

With less than a month before the season premiere was scheduled to air, the fans were getting excited, and speculation on the forums was starting to overrun even the most popular threads about re-runs, rumoured haunt sites, and infamously flimsy evidence. She smiled to herself when she saw OH_Boy's posts, right in the thick of things as usual, kicking off a thread he'd entitled NEW SEASON: WOOT.

Got a good feeling bout this season y'all – could even say i'm in good spirits. lol. =) Who's with me??

He'd had twenty-three responses within the hour, and eighty more since. Elsewhere, he'd answered a fan who had excitedly posted a blurry picture of the team unloading the van in her hometown: *Your very own OH sighting!! =) What's haunted where you are??*

That was only the start of it. Paolo had been busy, feeding the excitement. And apparently, she realized when she noticed the posting times, as sleepless as she had been: most of his posts were from the deep hours of the night. She texted him: *Whats w the nite of 1000 posts? Nxt time I cant sleep i'll text u instead – ur obvi awake.*

She had cruised through a few more fan postings before his response came in: *Do it. Im sure txting me'll solve ur sleepless problm.* She was about to reply when another message arrived: *btw, bf Ben's lovin this mtg. Tons of gadgets 4 new seasn. Brace urself 4 nonstop techtalk tonite.*

Jasmine frowned at the phone, her fingers hovering over the screen. Slowly, trying to answer her own question, she typed, *Ur at that mtg too? who else?*

He didn't reply.

From the far end of the table, her tablet burbled a video call alert. Jasmine saw her mother's smiling picture above the phone icon and sighed. She tapped the answer button as she gulped down the rest of her tea. Too late, she remembered that she couldn't handle that much liquid in one swallow anymore: the tepid muck lodged in her damaged throat like a brick in a drainpipe, and the sudden pain brought tears to her eyes.

Grunting with effort, she forced it down in pieces, dimly aware someone was calling to her.

"…Jasmine! *Jasmine!* Oh my God, are you choking?"

Jasmine waved a hand at the screen, shaking her head and blinking to clear her eyes. Her mother's panic subsided a little, but not her flow of words. "Sweetheart, are you all right? Are you in pain? Should I come over?"

Jasmine turned back to the screen long enough to roll her eyes, which was surprisingly difficult to do while wiping away the last of her tears. She shook her head while her mother's voice eased from concern to exasperation.

"Don't give me that look. I can see you're choking, you're clearly in distress, and when I ask what's wrong you don't say a word, so how –" She stopped herself with a little squeak, her face frozen in horror. "I – I only meant you're not signing anything. I didn't mean…"

She looked so flustered Jasmine took pity on her. Forcing herself to swallow again, she faced the screen full-on, waving her hand in a dismissive motion and mustering a smile. *Hi, Mom,* she signed, mouthing the words as well. *I'm fine. Really.*

As usual, her mother leaned closer to the screen, her eyes darting from Jasmine's mouth to her hands, as if determined not to miss a single detail. Message received, her mother sniffed, lifting a disbelieving eyebrow.

Drank too much tea, Jasmine signed next. Damn it, she couldn't remember the sign for 'swallow'. Her mother probably wouldn't know it anyway. *I'm fine.*

"Too much tea?" her mother said. "And that's what happened?"

Jasmine raised her hands and shoulders in an exaggerated shrug. Speaking with her mother was always a hodgepodge of bad charades and the ASL Jasmine had managed to learn so far. Whatever worked.

"What if you'd been all by yourself?"

I am by myself, Mom. And I'm fine.

"But… what if I hadn't been here? How would you have called for help? You don't even know your neighbours in that place. Where's Ben?

Could you reach him quickly if you needed to? Jassy, I know you said you were ready to go back to work, but remember that therapist suggested taking a whole year..."

Jasmine narrowed her eyes at the screen in warning. The therapist fiasco was off-limits, as her mother well knew. It had been awkward from minute one, and during the second session, when she'd hesitantly risked the team's non-disclosure agreement to talk about the Mortimer house, the guy had casually asked if Jasmine was taking any anti-psychotic medication. Her answer apparently hadn't convinced him, because he'd pulled Ben aside afterward to ask the same question. Jasmine had never seen Ben lose his temper so completely. Remembering that day made her stomach heave. Since then, they hadn't even talked about trying to find a new counselor.

Could be why she was still having nightmares, she reflected.

Her mother was still talking, trying to ward off another glare from Jasmine. "It's just, you've been through a lot and you're still healing. Going back to work is a big step, it'll put you right back into those same situations, and honey, anything could happen! You work alone, in the dark... I just don't know if it's such a good idea..."

Jasmine closed her eyes, listening to her mother fret on. It was the best way to weather this flood of maternal worry, and it helped her fight down the gut-twisting knowledge that they were all questions she'd asked herself in the aftermath of dreaming, more nights than not.

"I think it's going to be pretty awesome, actually," Ben was saying enthusiastically as they cleared dishes from the table.

Paolo's warning hadn't been far off. Ben had come home flustered, toting a dozen apology roses for forgetting to call and two aluminum equipment cases full of new toys for the season. The roses were in water on the dining room table; the cases were open on the living room floor, spewing cables and cameras and unidentifiable bits onto nearby furniture.

Ben's thoughts, too, were tumbling out in a cheerful heap. "If I can get a better look at all this tonight, I can give everyone an overview during the team meeting tomorrow, and we could probably start using them immediately. Plus, if the studio does go ahead with this new-recruit contest thing they're batting around, we'll need more equipment anyway. I guess we can test-drive these ones this season and see if they're things we'd want to trust amateurs with." He tore his gaze from the mess in the living room and beamed at her. She couldn't help but smile back.

Not sure about this contest, Jasmine signed. *Seems kind of gimmicky.* She had to spell the last one out, but they were both getting quicker at the ASL alphabet.

"Yeah, I know. It could be fun, but can you imagine the kind of applications someone's going to have to sift through to even find some candidates? Yikes." They exchanged horrified expressions as water filled the sink.

"Not our job, thank God," Ben went on, dropping plates into the soapy water. "Oh – and wait'll you see this camera Freddie sent us, a prototype he wants us to try, called a y-spectrum. I was like, what the hell's the y-spectrum? That's not even a thing. And he was all, 'oh, that's just the name, just go with it' – so I don't know, we'll see how it works. Maybe he can change the name." He looked at her. "It's lame, right? It's not just me."

Jasmine shook her head, then signed, *If it works, he should call it the Haunt-cam.*

"So then it's actually the H-spectrum." Ben's eyes lit up. "No: H-spectre-um! Right? Spectre?"

She mimed gagging. *Better idea: Polt-aroid.*

"Ooh, retro – good one." He grinned again, shaking a wet plate over the drainboard. "Or go even more classic: Spooker-8 camera!"

She laughed – another thing that just didn't work right anymore, all wheeze and squeak – and he leaned over to kiss her on the nose. It twisted his body awkwardly, his hands still in soapy water, but he stayed there a moment.

"Sorry," he said more softly, searching her face. "Not only did I forget to call, I'm technobabbling again, aren't I?"

Smiling, Jasmine held her thumb and index finger about an inch apart.

"I'm a dork," he sighed. "I suck."

Admitting it is half the battle.

He flicked a cloud of suds at her, which mostly disintegrated in mid-air, and she swatted him with the dishtowel. Then he turned back to the sink and started scrubbing again. "Okay, my turn to shut up for a while. How'd your day go?"

Her mouth actually opened as her fingers twitched into place, but then she noticed that, facing the sink, he wouldn't be able to see her reply. Jasmine stared blankly at his profile as the thought sank in. They'd worked out ways for her to get his attention, of course, light touches and signals that would look casual, natural to anyone watching. She'd just never had to use one in mid-conversation before.

It was bound to happen eventually, she thought. Lots of conversations happen when people aren't looking at each other. I'll just touch his arm, and it'll be fine. Or he'll look over. It'll be fine. It's not a disaster. Just deal with it.

Ben was still scrubbing dishes, not looking over. And even as she told herself sternly to cope, her hands started to shake. The moment stretched, filled only with the sounds of dishes bumping in water, and then she saw the realization finally hit him.

For a moment, Ben went utterly still. Then he twisted to face her again, dripping soap and water on the floor. "I'm so sorry. I didn't even think."

She nodded, not sure whether to laugh or cry, and tried a smile. She hung her teatowel carefully on its hook.

"Tell me about your day." He hesitated at her expression, then reached out a soapy hand. "Hey…"

The awkward smile felt glued to her mouth. Her shrug was a twitch that conveyed *not much, doesn't matter* and *don't touch me* all at once. She swallowed hard, tasting that morning's tea, and finally managed to sign a response. *I think I'll go to bed. Didn't sleep well last night.*

"Jasmine –"

I'm fine. But he didn't see it, because she was already walking away.

(卟)

"Give me the situation, Ben." Troy walked into camera frame and took up station behind Ben at the monitors, surveying the screens as if he'd been entirely absent during the afternoon's work of setting up cameras and sensors.

Ben launched gamely into his explanation of recorders and equipment placement. Jasmine's attention wandered. The tech briefing was part of every episode, but with her hospital time and the summer hiatus she'd somehow forgotten how crowded it always felt. Even in a large space like this one – they'd co-opted a dining hall, pushing remnants of broken furniture out of the way – it felt cramped, given the blockade of monitors and cables sprawled across three tables with all five team members on one side, and three cameramen, a sound operator, the field producer and his PA watching like silent birds of prey on the other. The real mystery each week, Jasmine reflected, wasn't the ghosts and spooky buildings: it was how the production crew made it seem as if the team was all alone in there.

She brought her focus back as Troy clapped Ben on the shoulder. "Good eyes, as always," he said. "Okay, everyone, looks like we're all set: the owners have given us the run of the place, so we're here on our own, and the weather's pretty tame outside – that should mean we don't have to worry about evidence contamination. If something goes bump in the night, it's either us or the spooks."

The team chuckled as if they'd never heard him say that before.

"All right. Assignments: Rachel and I are going to head up to that second floor guestroom, see whether the Colonel wants to come say hi to us tonight. Jas, why don't you stay here at the operations desk and take the first shift? Keep an eye on those other rooms and recorders for us, and text us a heads-up if you spot anything. Ben and Paolo, you head out to the courtyard with the thermal and the directional mic, see if you can pick up any of the action the client told us about."

Nods all around.

"That's it, folks. Watch your step, the floor's gone in places. Get what you need to stay safe, and stay in touch. Wheels up in five minutes."

Before anyone could move, Rachel's hand shot up as if in school. "Sir, I never got a wheel."

There was a startled silence, then people on both sides of the cameras burst out laughing.

"Cut! Rachel…" the producer sighed.

"What? It was funny. Leave it in."

"We can't keep it, Rache, half the crew laughed. Reset, everyone – let's go again."

"Oh, tosh," Rachel said breezily. "Who's going to notice a few extra voices in all that hilarity?"

Ben and the sound tech immediately protested that lots of people would notice, and as Rachel claimed not to believe them, Troy nudged Jasmine. "Hey," he said quietly. "You still okay with staying here at ops for the first shift?"

She stared at him, and signed in confusion: *That's what we agreed on.*

"I know, but…" He shrugged, looking uncomfortable. "I don't want you to feel like you're being pushed aside. You can head outside with Ben and leave Paolo here if you want."

"Hey," Paolo said.

"It's easy enough to change," Troy said, "since it looks like we'll be re-shooting at least part of this scene anyway." He tilted his head at the crowd around Rachel, who was nodding penitently at whatever the producer was saying. She caught Jasmine's eye and winked.

Jasmine hesitated, imagining the silent crumbling corners waiting upstairs and the debris-strewn courtyard outside. The bright lights of ops while they filmed this set-up scene were warm and comforting. She told her heart-rate to relax. *No*, she signed to Troy, hoping she looked calm and thoughtful. *I'm good here. I've got my tablet and Ben's already checked the connections, so I can reach you if I need to.* At least, that's what she tried to say. Eventually, she just held up her tablet and gave Troy a thumbs-up.

"You're sure?" Troy asked.

Yes. Nodding, she added phrases her hands knew by heart: *It's fine. I'm fine.*

"Okay," Troy said. When he turned back to his marker, Jasmine let out a breath before catching a glimpse of Ben's worried face. He'd already been gone when she'd woken in the hotel this morning, but five little x's made of bits of wire, thread, zip ties, dental floss and shredded take-out napkin had been waiting on his pillow. She managed a smile for him, but his expression hardly changed before he turned back to the monitors.

They all resumed their places for the second take. Jasmine listened to Troy detail the assignments again. Just keep giving readings, she thought, staring at the bank of monitors and speakers.

I can do that.

(ᵗᵇ)

By 4:52 a.m., Jasmine had decided the first case of the season was officially a bust. She'd spent three shifts at the monitors, watching and listening to all the feeds, increasingly bored as the night wound on. No matter how they were paired off or where they were sent, the team had found absolutely nothing by way of recorded responses, EMF spikes or even an unexpected breeze.

"Okay, that's it," Rachel's voice arrived just before she did. "I'm calling it. This place is dead – and not in a good way. It's disintegrating with every step, I have paint chips in my hair, and I've inhaled enough mold spores for a lifetime." She flung herself into a chair nearby and unwound her scarf.

Jasmine nodded. *Just thinking the same thing.*

"Great. Then you can take your eyes off those nothing-to-see-here monitors and pay attention to us for a while."

Startled, Jasmine looked up to see Paolo leaning against the doorframe. Rachel sat forward in her chair.

"Tell us what's going on with you."

Jasmine squinted at them, then shrugged at the monitors. She kept her ASL gestures slow and careful. *Nothing. I'm sitting here watching empty rooms.*

"Looking for a little more depth and honesty here, Jas," Rachel sighed.

"Lying to your teammates makes for a hostile work environment," Paolo said.

Jasmine frowned. *What is this?*

"Definitely not an intervention," Rachel said.

"Those are for bad reality TV," Paolo added. "We're classier than that."

"Indeed we are. Let's call it a situation report."

Too much Troy lately? Jasmine signed. *Get to the point.*

"I missed some of that," Paolo said, "but it looked cranky."

Rachel pointed a stern finger at Jasmine. "Don't make me tie your hands behind your back." While Jasmine blinked at her, she went on. "So here's the situation. You've taken more shifts at these damn screens tonight than I've ever seen you volunteer for, even though we're not getting so much as a shadow showing up anywhere." Her voice softened. "It seems like you're hiding."

"And you haven't volunteered to go anywhere alone," Paolo put in. "That's not like you."

"Ben said he offered to rig up a panic button, but you turned him down. Is that why you're playing it safe?"

Jasmine saw her mother's face, then the therapist's. She shook her head to banish them. *I'm not. I'm doing my job.*

"You're doing *a* job," Paolo said, "but not the one you usually do." *Someone has to watch the monitors.*

"Right," Rachel nodded, "but we take turns at it, to share the pain. No one expects you to do it all yourself."

"Okay," Paolo said. "Jas, have you been looking at the fan boards? Like, really looking? People are wondering about you. They're sympathetic about your 'illness' —"

"You should see some of the theories about that, by the way," Rachel put in. "Looks like those press releases were a waste of imagination."

"— but they want you investigating again. And frankly, tonight isn't going to convince them that you're back."

It's my first day! Jasmine protested, but her heart was thumping, and her mouth was dry. She dug her fingers into her thighs.

"Ah, you're easing into it," Rachel said. "So we can all expect to see you back to your usual self in the next episode?"

Sure, Jasmine nodded.

"Still not sleeping?" Paolo asked.

She narrowed her eyes at him and signed *Are you?,* but he didn't react.

"So that's it, is it?" Rachel said. "A few good nights' sleep, some good activity at the next sites, that's all you think you need? A few dark rooms and mysterious voices and you'll be back on side, good as new?"

"Easy peasy," Paolo said. "You should get right on that."

You bet, Jasmine signed, standing. *Thanks for the talk. I need some air.* Her urge to get outside felt instinctive, moving her toward the door without conscious thought.

"One more thing," Paolo said, pulling his phone from his pocket without moving from her path. "What with the lack of evidence in this place, we're going to need filler. We've already done a few segments of us talking about the new equipment and whatnot, but there is something else we could use." He started calling up something on his screen as he continued, more quietly than before. "We have these."

He showed her a photo she had to squint to see, but once she identified it, she flinched back in shock. *Where did you get that?*

"While you were in the hospital. Archivist, remember?" He flicked to the next photo, which showed her surgical scars in closer detail. She looked more dead than asleep, in that one. In the next, she was mostly hidden behind a forest of white coats and nursing scrubs around her bed. "It's not as creepy as it seems. Troy had me take them for insurance reasons. But we could use them to tell your story."

Her hand had risen to her throat without her even realizing it. The raised lines of her scars still felt alien and raw under her fingers.

"Not the whole story, and not the real one," Rachel said softly. "The stakeholders still don't want the Mortimer footage getting out. But the damage and your recovery are things we could consider sharing."

Jasmine turned to her, incredulous, feeling her scars stretch as she moved. *That's sick. It's... gruesome,* she mouthed. *And private.*

"It's your reality," Paolo said. "It shows how you fight, Jas, how far you've come." He flicked the screen again, and the next picture was her first meeting with the ASL tutor. Jasmine looked at her tiny self in the image, and remembered the terror building behind her polite mask. She remembered she'd thrown up her lunch so violently she'd thought for sure her stitches would re-open. She remembered she could hardly breathe that day.

No... no. She was shaking her head, and her scars were aching. *I have to go. I need... air.* She pushed Paolo out of the way and stumbled out, down a dark hallway with no plan or focus, distant voices calling her name. They faded as she fled.

When Paolo's pictures stopped whirling through her mind and she finally got her breathing and heart rate back under control, she found she was curled in a musty chair in a cramped bedroom. She was high enough that the moonlight came through the window clearly, so third or fourth floor at least, she thought. Muted activity downstairs told her the team was still on the job.

She pulled her legs closer, sending dust motes up to gleam in the thin light, and tried to borrow calm from the pale moon outside.

After a while, footsteps in the hall made her sigh. If they're looking for me, they'll have to actually come in, she thought tiredly. It's not like I'll answer if they call my name.

"Hmph," a quiet voice said. "Thought I saw someone come up here."

She glanced up, but couldn't see anyone yet. A floorboard creaked in the doorway.

"Can't blame anyone for wanting a bit of peace," the voice grumbled. "The way people carry on. Tramping through here at all hours, asking their questions and reading numbers off machines. Where's the sense?"

Jasmine kept very still. She sent her eyes to every corner and shadow, seeing no change. The voice sounded faint and scratched, like an old man whispering in an empty church, but it was also quite definitely inside the room with her.

Her gaze fixed on the bed. The grimy mattress flattened along one edge, as if someone had sat down on it.

"Inviting just anyone nearby to show up and talk? Fool idea," the voice went on. "Never know what might answer, and then what'll you do? If I had a message I'd have told someone years ago." A faint but distinctive sigh sounded as the dust motes drifted again. "And now some girl's playing Goldilocks, sitting in my chair. Never ends."

Jasmine pushed her feet to the floor and stood as quickly as she could. *Sorry*, she mouthed. *I'll leave.*

There was a pause, a sensation almost like the room held its breath for a moment, then the voice sounded again, suspiciously. "Can you hear me, girlie?" At Jasmine's nod, a shorter pause descended. "Hmph. And you're so scared the cat's got your tongue?" The low chuckle crept across her skin.

Jasmine had just started to shake her head when she heard a floorboard creak right in front of her. She had the abrupt sensation of someone standing very close, and the hair on her arms stood on end.

"I appreciate the courtesy," the scratched old voice whispered, distant in her ear. "But I'd prefer it if you and your friends left now. It's been a long night, having them tramp around everywhere, calling at me."

Nodding, Jasmine turned carefully in place and headed for the door, determined not to run.

"You come back another time, though, girlie," the voice called as she crossed the threshold. "I like your approach."

She didn't even notice the dark of the hallway, stepping around the rotten floorboards without thinking to find her way to the top of the stairs. Her mind was churning as she started down. She reached ops a few moments later, blinking in the sudden light, and found Troy, Ben and the crew packing up the equipment.

When Ben looked up, his face cleared immediately. "There you are. Thank God. Are you all right?"

She nodded, slid both arms around his startled shoulders, and kissed him.

"Well," Troy said. "Good thing the cameras weren't rolling. That'd be a pretty big reveal for the season premiere."

"At least it'd fill some time," the producer said glumly.

Jasmine held Ben's surprised gaze with her own, ensuring he didn't look away. *I'm sorry,* she mouthed, and spelled it out between them so only he could see. *And I am not fine. But I'm going to try to get better.*

His surprise slid into confused worry.

Aw, bless him.

She kissed him briskly, took her tablet out of his hands, opened her notes program and started typing, wishing the crew were better at ASL. I'll have to keep this with me all the time, she thought as the pack-up resumed around her. Or get a stylus and write on it directly, that'd be faster. Get Ben to find me a good text-to-speech conversion program. And I have to remember to carry a pad of paper with a pencil as back-up... very old school. Mom will approve.

She planted herself in the middle of the room and whistled sharply – at least she could still do that. All three men peered at the tablet screen as Jasmine smiled.

Don't give up on this ruin just yet. I'll need permission to come back on my own tomorrow, and some on-camera time back at the studio.

Someone's going to have to be the strong silent type, she thought. Guess it might as well be me.

Technical Support

He suddenly realized someone was calling his name.

"Oh Ben, you *are* here," Joyce said with feigned surprise as she stuck her head around the doorframe.

"Sorry. I was working." He waved his soldering iron as evidence.

"Right. Is that whatever-it-is nearly ready? Client's going to be here around three o'clock to pick it up."

"It's an electromagnetic field detector that runs into the radio range." Ben checked his watch. "And it's only just past two. It'll be ready."

"Better be – they may be weirdos with weird toys but at least they pay their bills."

"What's the matter, boss?" Freddie put in, clattering through parts on his workbench. "Don't you believe in ghosts?"

She ignored him. "I'm heading out on an install. Call the work phone if you need me." She disappeared into the front room.

Ben moved his magnifier over the last quadrant of the circuit board and smiled at the discoloured patch on a transistor. "Gotcha." Moving quickly, he melted the old solder connections, removed the hot pieces with quick, precise motions of the suction pump, and tweezed the transistor out of place. "That's what you get for not doing your job," he murmured as he dumped it into his bits bin and chose a new one from the stock.

"Huh?"

"Nothing." Ben clamped the transistor in place, then dabbed flux around the connection points. He cleaned the tip of his soldering iron, uncoiled a silvery strand of solder from its roll, and deftly dabbed on the new connections. As he straightened, he rolled his shoulders back to get the cramp out of them and waved the last wisps of smoke toward his venting fan.

Keeping an eye on the time, he snugged the whole circuit board back into place in its casing and tidied his workbench. Then he grabbed the detector's back plate and stood up. "I'm going to go wait out front in case she – in case they show up early."

Freddie made little kissing noises.

"Shut up," Ben muttered. He kicked the leg of Freddie's desk as he passed.

Freddie laughed, lifting his soldering iron. "I bet you believe in ghosts, huh, Benny boy?"

"What does that have to do with anything?" Pulling out the front desk stool made enough noise to drown out Freddie's reply, but Ben didn't care.

In the quiet of the front room, he re-assembled the casing and tightened the screws on the back plate. Studying the finished product, he noticed the wear scratches on all the corners and the gauge window. This EMF detector wasn't pretty, but it was functional and easy to read. He switched it on and watched the needle quiver slightly in the low, green range. That had been all it could do when it first landed on his desk, wrapped in a work order.

Ben held the device toward the check-out monitor and watched the needle climb, then watched it fall as he moved it away. Standing, he headed for the display of re-furbished laptops, watching the needle swing decidedly into the middle and higher ranges, edging the dial's orange zone. Then he looked around, trying to remember what his conscious brain had hardly noticed during his six months' working here – ah, there it was: the circuit breaker panel in the far corner, next to the ancient mini-fridge marked "For Employee Use ONLY!!".

Even as he approached, the needle jumped, waving wildly for a moment before settling into the corner of the red zone. He smiled. "Gotcha."

"Good thing that isn't right next to your workbench," an amused voice said from just behind him.

Ben whirled, the detector nearly sliding out of his grip.

"Sorry," said the newcomer. "Didn't mean to startle you. Hi." Her smile lit the room.

He got his mouth working again just as she went on.

"Well, isn't this a coincidence," she said, pointing at the device in his hand, "because I'm pretty sure that's mine. Or ours, I guess. I'm –"

"Rachel," he said, nodding. "Yes, I knew you'd come. Today. For this. Which is yours, you're right." *You know, this is why Joyce prefers you don't speak to customers.* The knowing commentator at the back of his mind was familiar: it had spoken up on his first day here, offering reminders about professional behaviour and how he couldn't afford to lose this job. Ben shut his mouth firmly and headed for the front counter.

"I know I'm a little early," Rachel was saying. "But I came in, saw you there and just thought, really, how many EMF detectors could they be fixing at one time? So I took a chance."

"Right, yeah. Good. Um, was there a box with this, or…?"

"Are you kidding?" She laughed. It was so genuine it almost made him laugh himself. She had nice teeth. "If there ever was, it's long gone. We used to keep most of our gear in fishing tackle boxes, if you can believe that, but we're finally moving up in the world enough to spring for hard-sided suitcases with foam inserts. It always makes us look like we're smuggling illegal weapons or something. And putting everything away at the end of a job is like 3-D Tetris on multiplayer mode. So, a box? No. This one will just have to slum it in my bag for a while until I get can get it tucked in with the others." She dropped her purse on the counter and held out a hand.

Ben blinked at her as if she'd been speaking another language. *Doesn't matter. Give it back.* He placed the device carefully in her palm.

"Great. Thanks." She shoved it into her purse with hardly a glance and dug out her wallet while he winced. "And at least I know for a fact that it works – saw it pegged in the red while you were over there in the corner."

"It works," Ben confirmed, trying not to sound defensive. "I wouldn't give it back to you if it didn't."

She looked up from her wallet and studied him a moment. "No, you wouldn't, would you?"

Say something professional. He turned to the register. "Parts and labour… $17.50."

"Still the best deal in town." She handed him a twenty. "Thanks again. And, just a tip: I'd stay away from that corner as much as possible." She nodded toward the corner. "With those kinds of readings, you've got a pretty intense field over there."

Let it go, the career coach in his head said sternly. *The customer is always right.* But Ben couldn't let that sort of comment pass. "Well. It's above the usual ambient EM level, true. But it's still within human tolerance."

It was her turn to blink at him for a moment before speaking. "Depends on what you mean by 'tolerance', I guess," she said. "I mean, sure, it won't tear your skin cells open or boil the blood in your veins. But a lot of people start feeling uncomfortable at about a tenth the level that thing is kicking out."

"A tenth is hardly anything," Ben said. He waved a hand around the shop. "Cumulatively, the leakage from all this would likely equal what we saw over there."

"Ah, that's spread over a whole room. The problem shows up in concentrated areas, like that one. If you had your workbench over there for hours every day, you'd see what I mean, believe me. And in a few years, probably, so would your oncologist."

Was her voice slightly less friendly than it had been? He thought so.

Okay, now let it go, his inner advisor recommended. *So she's wrong. It's not a big deal.*

"I don't think so," Ben said, and her smile dimmed. "Freddie and I probably have a higher-than-average field in the tech room back there, and we work just fine for hours every day."

"Are you talking about me?" Freddie appeared in the doorway, blowing gently on a circuit board. He saw Rachel and stopped. "Oh. Hi. Sorry to interrupt."

"Freddie," Ben said, "what do you think the background EM reading would be back there, with everything running?"

"We could easily find out," Rachel put in. "Seeing as how I've got this cool little gizmo for it and everything." She lifted the detector, and Ben reached for it without thinking. "Nuh-uh," she said, holding it close. Her eyes met his in what seemed to be amused challenge. "You're trying to support your own theory. If I let you work this, anything you say would be highly suspect. You could skew the results. Have you ever heard of something called confirmation bias?"

"Of course," Ben said. His career coach harrumphed grumpily at her look of surprise. "But I don't see how I could possibly bias results on a device like this. I can't physically touch the needle, and it's not as if I could spontaneously create or remove an electromagnetic field in a room to influence the reading."

"You know the space, and you know what's nearby," Rachel insisted. "Plus, you just fixed this machine – or claimed you did. I, on the other hand, don't have any idea what this so-called tech room is like, so I have no range of possible results in mind. I'm an unbiased user."

Unbiased. Ha! "Even without seeing the room, you could make some logical assumptions about what's back there and have a number range in mind. Then we'd be proving your theory."

"But I would face the same problems you do in physically influencing this machine – it's not like I can change the reading just with the awesome power of my brain." She beamed at him again.

She's trying to distract you! "Then we'll use Freddie," Ben said, turning away.

Holding the circuit board in front of him like a shield, Freddie looked from Ben to Rachel. "What are we talking about?"

"It's very simple," Rachel assured him. "We want you to take this EMF detector —" she deftly swapped the circuit board in his hands for the device "— hold it just like that, and walk into the tech room with it. Then we're all going to watch what happens to this little gauge needle."

"It measures the strength of the electromagnetic fields around you," Ben added.

"Oh yeah," Freddie said. "I used something like this in school. Okay."

"Wait," Rachel said suddenly. "Am I allowed back there? Because you know I'm going to need to see the scan in person to accept the results."

The two men looked at each other. *Clients are definitely not allowed in the work area,* Ben's advisor reminded him.

"I'm sure it'll be fine," Ben said, giving Freddie a meaningful frown.

"Dude, please," Freddie snorted. "Let's do this."

Ben had just enough time to notice, as Rachel came around the counter to stand beside him and Freddie, that she was shorter than he'd thought, and she smelled like vanilla.

They shuffled into the tech room as an awkward trio.

The needle blurred into motion as they moved past the workbenches to the center of the room. There they all stopped and watched as the needle settled, trembling, in the red zone.

"Hmm. Look at that," Rachel murmured, more than a hint of satisfaction in her voice. Then she looked around. "This is where you work all day?"

Ben was still staring at the needle. *That can't be right.* "Most of the day."

"How high does this thing go?" Freddie hadn't taken his eyes off the needle as he waved the machine from left to right. "Red's not good, is it? Was it green out there?" He spun and paced away, muttering, into the front room.

Rachel was still studying the work area. "You sure you don't feel anything out of the ordinary in here?"

"Stiff muscles from sitting too long," Ben replied, "and the occasional solder burn. I don't understand why it's so high. I wouldn't have thought these things were emitting those kinds of levels, even cumulatively."

"Well, apparently they are. Cumulative and concentrated, actually, since it's so cozy in here." She looked around again. "Are you sure this isn't a closet?"

"Maybe there's a calibration problem."

She raised her eyebrows again. "It's a pretty simple device. How would it get miscalibrated?"

His mind was already racing, suggesting and discarding ideas. *That reading can't be right.* "I don't know," he admitted. "Could you leave it with me again? I'll figure out some tests."

"I guess I can," she said, "but I'd need it for Friday at the latest. We're out of town on a case this weekend and that'll mean all hands on deck. We have two others like it, but…"

"I can have it done for Friday."

"Okay, then." Her touch on his arm made him notice her frown. "You should consider another explanation – other than equipment failure."

"Oh my God, are we haunted?" Freddie reappeared, sounding torn between amusement and worry.

"Always a possibility," Rachel said with a faint smile at him before turning back to Ben. "I think it's more likely that the wiring in this room isn't as shielded as it should be. You're working in a fear cage, and that's no good for anyone."

"Fear cage?" Freddie's laugh sounded strained.

"Room this size, inadequate ventilation, fluorescent light, high EMF: that is a textbook fear cage. At these levels," Rachel pointed at the device, "you'd probably start feeling as if you were being watched all the time. You'd get headaches, maybe feel dizzy and confused, tire easily…"

Ben stared at her. "I never feel any of that."

"I do!" Freddie said, his eyes wide. "I figured it was just, you know, being at work."

"And it could be." Rachel shrugged, taking the EMF detector from him and giving it to Ben. "But I've been in here for what, maybe two minutes? Not even? And already I'm feeling uncomfortable. Twitchy, and the back of my neck is crawling. Look." She raised an arm. "Goosebumps."

That reading can't be right. "Psychosomatic," Ben offered, feeling he should comfort her somehow. "You've seen the numbers, so your body thinks it should react."

She rubbed her arm. "Maybe. I'm also sensitive to EMF levels. It's not like I could predict what the readings are without a sensor, but I can tell you when it's not healthy. And this? This isn't healthy. You need to tell your manager. Call an electrician. Something."

Ben followed her back into the front room, noticing how her shoulders eased as she neared the front door. "Are you okay?" he asked.

She smiled, seeming almost as cheerful as when she'd arrived. "Meh, nothing I'm not used to. So… Friday?"

"Yes," Ben said. "And if it is a calibration problem, maybe you should test your other sensors as well."

"That's probably a good idea anyway. It's not like they've had a check-up since Troy bought them. Heck, none of our equipment has, and we've got boxes of the stuff."

"Suitcases," he said, trying for humour.

"Right, suitcases now." She chewed her lip a moment. "What are you doing this weekend?"

His mind went utterly blank and silent for a moment, and by the time it all came rushing back, she was digging in her purse. Automatically, he took what she handed him before glancing down to see.

"Operation: Haunting," he read aloud.

"Yeah, it's kind of a goofy name, right? It was Troy's idea, because he –" She waved a hand. "Doesn't matter. The point is: you're good with gadgets and we have a bunch that probably need work. You're methodical, logical. It's true you do argue with me, but I'm willing to overlook that…"

"I didn't – I wasn't really arguing as such –"

"Don't interrupt, you'll make it worse." Grinning, she went on. "You also seem to have a huge tolerance for EMF, which could be useful. So I have just two questions."

"Okay…"

"First: what's your name?"

"Oh! Ben. I'm Ben." *Handshake. Be professional.* He stuck out a hand, awkwardly, and she took it.

"Hi, Ben, nice to meet you. Second: do you believe in ghosts?"

He pulled his hand back. "What does that have to do with anything?"

She paused, then laughed her infectious laugh again. "You know what? Nothing. Call that number tomorrow, and if I'm not there, talk to Troy. I think we should negotiate a full technical check-up before this weekend's case. Whether we do it before we leave or once we're on site would have to be something we work out with the accountants."

"On site?"

"Yeah, we're in Vermont this weekend. Do you ski at all?" She snickered at his expression. "I'm kidding. Well, sort of. We really are going to Vermont, though." She wrapped her scarf around her throat and took hold of the doorknob. "Look, I don't know what the budget would be like for this, but I'll talk to Troy and do what I can. First, because no one with your mind should be frying it daily in there –" she pointed at the back room "– and second… because you seem like you'd be a really handy guy to have around, Ben."

She treated him to one more smile and walked out into the afternoon, letting a blast of autumn air inside to take her place.

ф

It had been a week of firsts, Ben reflected as he opened the car door: finally meeting Rachel in person, letting a client into a restricted area, insisting Joyce call an environmental assessor for the tech room, fudging a work order to get off-site for the day. "Really? They want you, personally?" Joyce had asked skeptically; "Go get 'er, tiger!" Freddie had whispered.

Ben shivered in the morning chill and looked up at the modest sign above the shop before him. At least there wasn't a cartoon ghost with a circled red slash through it, he thought. Taking a deep breath, he stepped from the frosty parking lot to a warm beige room with a basic reception desk and a pair of brown chairs.

"Ben?" A tall, broad-shouldered man came striding out from behind the desk when Ben nodded. "I'm Troy. Glad you could make it."

"Me, too. Thanks. For this opportunity, I mean." *Handshake,* his career coach reminded him.

"Heck, it's something we probably should've done long ago. I'm glad Rachel found you. Come on in, we're just through here."

They went down a short narrow hallway to stop at a room filled mostly with an old dining table and chairs, only one of which was occupied.

"Hey, Ben," Rachel said as she looked up. "You made it. Have a seat – we're still waiting for Paolo. He claims he's caught in traffic."

Ben looked around for any technology in need of fixing, but besides the laptop in front of Rachel, there was only a water barrel with a crown of paper cups, and a yellowing plant by the window. "I should probably just get started," he said. "Is there an equipment room, or…?"

Rachel smiled knowingly at Troy. "Told you."

He sighed. "Fine, lunch is on me. As usual. Come on, Ben, I'll show you where you can set up."

The door across the hallway opened into a room with floor-to-ceiling shelves along one wall and a battered metal desk and chair near the window. Three large hard-sided suitcases were piled by the door. Ben stood for a moment, taking in the shelves full of wires and cords, black plastic casings, and the occasional dull metal plate reflecting the light back at him.

Hmm, commented his career advisor. *It's like a playground.* Then he realized Troy was speaking.

"…to handle in one visit. I'd suggest you prioritize. Everything we'll need this weekend should be here in these suitcases." He squinted at the shelves, frowning. "And all that should be better organized. I swear, I take a few days off and the place just falls apart." He sighed and moved toward the shelves.

Ben felt himself smiling as he put his work kit on the chair and reached for the first suitcase.

"Just be careful as you lift those cases. They're –" At the sound of the latches springing open, Troy turned around to see the suitcase already on the table, Ben lifting the lid eagerly. "– heavier than they look."

Ben looked up. "Is this a thermal imaging camera?" At Troy's nod, he wedged it carefully out of its foam pocket and turned it over in his hands, nodding. "Pretty much like the one I saw online."

"Oh? Are you in the market for one?"

"No, no. I did some research so I'd know what I might be dealing with. Rachel gave me a partial list over the phone, but she didn't have models or serial numbers." He squinted at the faded printing on the power pack.

"We have some pretty specialized devices," Troy said doubtfully. "We should still have the instruction manuals around here if you run into something you can't manage."

"I'll be fine," Ben said as politely as he could. *Laughing at the client is unprofessional.* "Their component parts will be pretty standard: inductors, capacitors, integrated circuits on printed circuit boards… anything that will register, conduct or manipulate electromagnetic energy. The only real variations show up in how they're powered, what kind of energy fields they recognize, and how they express that to us. Oh, that reminds me." He opened his kit and pulled out the EMF detector. "This is working fine. Should I test your other ones first? I've got a pretty conclusive set of calibration checks now."

Belatedly he noticed the look on Troy's face, and in the moment of silence he mentally replayed what he'd said. *What did you do wrong? Were you unprofessional?* But then the corners of Troy's mouth turned upwards, and the moment passed.

"Good idea. They should be in there somewhere, actually." He gestured to the suitcase and its jumbled wires. "And again, I apologize. That should be a lot neater."

"That's okay. I brought extra ties." Ben reached through the tangle and pulled up an EMF detector. "Is it okay if I write on these?"

"Write on them?"

"With white grease pencil. It'll rub off later," he added quickly, "but it helps me keep track of what I've already dealt with, especially since I see sets of duplicates here."

"Sure," Troy said, his eyes on the power cord Ben was wrapping into a deft figure eight. "Knock yourself out. We're just next door if you need anything."

Ben didn't even hear him leave.

⟨⊞⟩

"Whoa. I don't think I've ever seen this place so organized. And that is really saying something, with Troy around."

Ben looked up at the familiar voice. "Oh. Hi, Rachel. Let me just finish this." He set the final casing screw into place with one hand and reached for the screwdriver with the other.

"*Oh hi Rachel,* he says. I've lost my mystique already." She sounded amused, but he didn't look up again. "You know you've been in here for almost three hours, right?"

"Mmm." Ben swapped the screwdriver for the grease pencil and made a small notation on the back plate, then straightened to stretch. He noticed Rachel expectantly standing in the doorway. "Did you say something?"

"Break time." He started to protest, but she narrowed her eyes. "Step away from the desk and come with me."

"I still have half a suitcase to do," he protested as he followed her across the hall. *Don't antagonize the client, but try to get away as soon as you can.*

Troy and a younger man were sitting at the table, behind a platter of sub sandwiches and a scattering of paper. Both looked up, and Troy waved Ben into the room. "Ben, Paolo. Paolo, this is Ben."

Paolo nodded. "Nice to meet you. I did stick my head in when I arrived, but you were elbow-deep in something and didn't hear me."

"Sorry," Ben said. "I was working."

"Understood. I can get pretty focused when I'm on a project, too."

"Really?" Rachel asked. "I've seen no evidence of that phenomenon."

"Have a seat, Ben, and help yourself," Troy said, nodding at the plate. "You've done a huge job in there already, thanks. Any major problems we should know about?"

Careful. Just gloss. Words of one syllable. "Nothing major, no. I replaced a few parts and wires for you and cleaned the dust out of the casings. If too much gets into some of the more sensitive components it can affect your readings." Rachel was pushing the plate of food at him, so he took half a sub to be polite. "But if you're going to Vermont this weekend, you may have a different issue."

They looked at him in surprise.

"The cold," he said. "You work at night, right? Will you be very far north? Are you going to be outside for very long with your equipment, or anywhere it might get wet?"

"No," Paolo said. "It's an indoor job."

"Indoor, but abandoned," Rachel said thoughtfully. "For more than five years now, so I doubt the power's still on or the furnace running. How bad a shape is it in? Do we have pictures or anything?"

They all reached for pages and started scanning while Ben bit into his sub and realized how hungry he was. "Do you mind if I ask what the site is?" he asked, trying not to speak with a mouthful.

"It's an old B&B. Here's the latest real estate listing," Paolo said.

"That'll just tell us it's a charming fixer-upper," Rachel muttered. "There's got to be something more."

"You could try Google Earth and street-view it." When they all stared at him, Ben went back to his sandwich. "Just a suggestion."

Paolo pulled the laptop closer and started typing.

"The cold might not matter too much," Troy said. "We can run heaters off the generator if we have to. Plus the TV crew's lights will keep the operations desk pretty warm and cozy."

"This is being televised?" Ben asked.

"And it's not even our first time," Paolo said. "This will be our second annual live Hallowe'en special." He didn't sound especially enthusiastic.

"And maybe, if we're really lucky and it all goes well…" Rachel nudged Troy.

"Don't count your chickens," the older man warned.

"Yeah, you'll jinx it," Paolo muttered, staring at the screen. "That'd be a shame."

"I wouldn't sound so smug there, sunshine. I don't know if we should even allow you to be on TV again."

Ben looked from one to the other.

"Whatever," Paolo sighed. "It was fine."

"Uh, no. Viewers were evenly split between loving you and hating you," Rachel corrected him.

"I was nervous!"

"We were all nervous," Troy said, moving to look over Paolo's shoulder.

"Not me. They loved me," Rachel said.

Paolo rolled his eyes. "Everyone loves you."

"Okay," Troy said. "So the satellite view shows part of the roof is gone, at least, and this image is – what? – two years old, so it could be worse by now. Street view…" He shook his head when Paolo finished clicking. "It's set pretty far back and through some trees, but that bank of windows doesn't look intact to me."

"Agreed." Paolo frowned at the screen. "Pack your parkas."

"And some blankets for the equipment," Ben added, earning another round of stares. "Draping the suitcases should help insulate them and maybe cut down on any condensation problems as you move between warm and cold. You might also find the batteries don't last as long. Some of them are sensitive to near- and sub-zero temperatures."

"Sounds like batteries are going to be the issue this trip anyway," Paolo sighed. "Reports from the last tenants and the local ghost hunters say that power drain is a problem. It's one of the most consistent claims."

"A whole night of running back and forth for new batteries," Rachel said. "Good cardio, at least."

Ben was frowning at Paolo. "What do you mean, power drain?"

"Just what it sounds like. The equipment won't run as long. You can go in there with a full charge and have everything just shut down fifteen minutes later." Paolo smiled a little when he saw Ben's doubtful expression. "Truth. I've seen it happen."

"Faulty battery."

"No," Troy said. "The most popular theory is that spirits will borrow energy from any available source to help them manifest. So the more active a site is, the more power it drains from our equipment."

"Operator error, then."

"Nope. The power just disappears."

Ben looked over at Rachel, but couldn't find her usual mischievous mood. He turned back to the two men. "That isn't how it works. Power doesn't disappear. It can be transferred or transformed, but it doesn't just disappear."

"Then I guess it gets transferred," Paolo shrugged.

"To… a ghost." *Don't be sarcastic with the clients!*

"Yeah, so it can knock on walls, speak on our recorders, show itself…" Rachel said, then stopped. "You don't believe us."

Ben stood, feeling disappointed. "I'll go finish that suitcase and get out of your way."

He was sitting at the desk with the back of a thermal camera half-unscrewed, when Paolo came in carrying a chair and a laptop.

"They asked me to prove it," Paolo said, dropping the chair the chair beside Ben. "Archivist to the rescue." He started mousing through screens and selected a file. "Here," he said, with a final swipe of the cursor. "Listen to this. It's from a team in upstate New York. They're in the ballroom of an old hotel."

Ben stifled a sigh and kept working at the camera casing, but the laptop was so close he couldn't help but listen. In his peripheral vision, soundwaves looped and danced over the screen.

"– back soon," an unfamiliar voice said, echoing slightly through the speakers. "Hope they're having better luck than we are. There's not so much as a twitch on this dang thing. Maybe if we head back to the main staircase again –"

"Uh, Chuck? My camera just –" Then the two voices called out in alarm, and in the jumble of exclamations that followed, Ben concluded both their flashlights had just gone dark.

"Shut up for a sec," one voice finally said. "I thought I heard something… Is someone here with us?" The echo died away and the speakers hissed for a while, then a solid thud sounded in the distance.

"Did you borrow our power so you can talk to us?" the second voice called. "We don't mind, you just startled us. Try to make another noise so we know you're here."

Three knocks, like a closed fist on wood, drifted through the speaker.

"That was from here in this room," the first voice whispered excitedly.

Sighing, Ben reached over and hit the stop button. "Their camera died first, I gather. So there's no video with this?"

"Right."

"Do you have a second audio file from elsewhere in the room, to compare this to? Or a third? Something that might help you triangulate the source of the knock?"

"No, just this."

"So in fact, that knock could be anything. Up to and including those two doing it themselves." He turned back to the thermal camera's innards.

Paolo was silent for a moment, then started calling up more files. "Okay, then. Video it is. We got this from Vancouver – it includes a second, confirmatory source."

"I'm not sure 'confirmatory' is a word."

"Whatever. Look."

Paolo arranged the screen so that two video feeds from a large, ornate theatre played side-by-side: one camera was onstage, trained out toward the cavernous audience area, where a young woman stood in the nearest aisle, filming the stage. The other video feed was from her perspective, featuring the stage and the grinning woman standing there with her own camera. When Paolo clicked play, each camerawoman started waving and a flood of laughter came from the speakers.

"Finally here! Hi!" the one onstage called, echoing strangely as both her microphone and her friend's relayed her voice through the computer speakers. "We've got about two hours to curtain and I'm pretty sure I should be doing something else right now!"

"This theatre is unbelievably gorgeous," the other woman was saying, starting to pan around the walls.

"Keep your eye on the power levels," Paolo said to Ben, pointing at the upper corners of each feed. The camera onstage showed a full charge; the other was about three-quarters full.

"... got the original designer to oversee the renovation. How often does that happen?" the woman standing in the aisle was saying, as the one onstage did a hammy softshoe dance. The onstage camera jiggled in time with the dancer's movements, then abruptly went black.

"Oops, hang on," the one onstage said, her voice now distant, coming only from the audience camera. "I think I just turned my camera off."

"Nice job, doofus!" chortled her friend, zooming as the woman onstage peered at her own camera. "Hey, look, it's like you have your own spotlight. That's so cool!" She zoomed back to show a haze of glowing bluish light just above her friend's shoulder.

The light flickered to the side as the woman onstage turned. Then it shrunk into a baseball-sized orb, darted to the back of the stage, and disappeared. The woman in the audience gasped. "Was that... was that your camera flash?"

"No. It's dead," the woman onstage said, holding it up, and Paolo paused the image of her startled face.

"Operator error," Ben said, turning back to his work. "She was dancing and excited, and she hit the power button."

"No, because that particular model takes a moment to power down, and we would've heard the power-off sound through the other camera's audio feed, and seen the lens retract. But that one just died. With a full charge."

"Faulty battery, or a faulty connection, then. That would shut everything down in an instant. Nothing left to retract the lens with."

"Then what was the ball of light?"

Ben looked at him in disbelief. *Is this some sort of test?* "It's obviously a functioning theatre. It would have a full lighting rig with all kinds of spotlights and filters, along with professionals who know how to use them."

"There was no one else there. You did notice that shot from the stage, with the utter lack of people...?"

"There was no one else we could see in the audience area. But someone might've been behind a pillar or crouched behind the seats somewhere. In any case, the lighting rig and catwalks would be well above the stage. We couldn't see those at all from either view."

Paolo stared at him again for a few seconds. "Okay. One more."

Ben turned back to work. His inner career coach sighed for him. *Maybe Joyce is right and they are weirdos. Don't say that aloud.*

"Okay," Paolo said again. "You watch this – I have to go get something." He pressed play and left the room.

Almost despite himself, Ben looked over and immediately recognized Rachel on screen, though she was oddly alien: an all-over greyish green with pale hair and disconcerting white pupils that seemed to be looking right at him. *Night vision camera. Interesting.* He pulled the laptop closer.

"Dynes Conservatory of Music," Troy's voice murmured from the speaker. "2:17am. I've got the night vision and an EMF detector; Rachel's got the still camera and a voice recorder."

"We need to build some kind of harness or something. I'm juggling stuff here like I'm in Cirque du Soleil," Rachel muttered.

"I'm sure you'll manage." Troy's camera panned slowly around a large room, lighting up the rows of chairs and a podium. A chalkboard flared for a moment on the wall as the camera passed, and the corners of the room were dense with shadow. After a full circle with no other movement or person in sight, the camera returned to Rachel, surrounded by empty chairs.

"It's not right that a music room should be so silent," she said, then raised her voice. "Hello? Is anyone here?" She paused for a moment, but there was only stillness. "We've come to hear some music. Would you play for us? Or sing?" She stopped to listen again.

"Was that a piano I just heard?" Troy murmured.

"I didn't hear anything," she whispered back.

Neither did I, thought Ben, but then Rachel stiffened and looked behind her. When she didn't move again, Troy hissed, "What?"

"The air changed," she said softly, turning back to stare with wide white pupils. "Something's different."

"You're sure?"

"Believe me - it's like the test my dad gave me on my eighth birthday, and it's making my skin crawl. Just check the EMF."

Troy raised the device into his camera's view and zoomed in until the gauge was visible. "Still only reading a four. They must've wired this room for sound. Wait." The needle was twitching, then jumped. "Five now. Seven. Nine – seven again."

In the background, Rachel was rubbing the base of her skull. "Yeah, like I said. Who's here with us? Can you tell us your name?" She held up the voice recorder and turned in a slow circle.

A little cartoon battery, outlined in red, started flashing in the top corner of the screen. Troy muttered, "We're going to lose power. I swear, I just charged th—" The picture and its audio fuzzed once, then faded back into view, jostling as Troy fumbled. "—voice recorder," he said, and Rachel handed it over.

Lifting the still camera, she started taking pictures, turning in a circle as she did.

"Are you still here? If you need power," Troy was saying, "why not take it from –"

The screen went blank.

"I was going to say 'one of us'," the real Troy said from the doorway of the equipment room. "Actually, I did say that. But no one took me up on it."

"Faulty battery," Ben said.

"Thank you for assuming I know how to work the equipment, at least. No accidental switch offs for me," Troy said, amused. He crossed to the table and dropped a photo in front of Ben. "That's the supplemental evidence for that case."

Ben picked it up carefully. In it, Troy was examining the night-vision camera, shoulders slumped inward in frustration. To his left was a tall, pale woman. Her features were blurred, but her expression radiated impatience in a way Ben couldn't describe. Her dark hair was up in a severe bun, her collar tight to her throat, her sleeves puffed at the shoulders, and her skirt dissolved into tendrils of cloudy shadows two feet from the ground. He could see the chairs in rows behind her.

"Who is this?" Ben asked.

Troy shrugged. "Never got a name."

"Rachel saw this? You saw this?"

"Nope," the other man said, dropping into the chair Paolo had vacated. "Just the camera."

Ben stared at the photo, studying the edges of the woman's form. "Photoshop," he said.

Troy laughed. "You saw the state of this room when you got here, and you're the one who suggested Google Street View. You really think any of us are savvy enough to Photoshop something like this?" When Ben opened his mouth to protest, Troy held up a hand. "Let me guess: we could pay someone to do it."

Ben nodded, and Troy sighed.

"Okay, that's true. But humour me for a minute. Begin with this set of ideas: the battery was fine, I used the equipment properly, and no one doctored the record."

Ben frowned at him, then back at the photo. He realized that what he had thought was a fold in the woman's blouse was actually Troy's elbow, visible through her torso.

"What happens if you accept that as real?" Troy asked. "Does it change who you are or what you do? All it does is support what you said earlier: that energy is never lost – it is merely transferred."

"From your camera battery... to the ghost."

"In this case, yeah. Like jump-starting a car. In other places it doesn't work like that. I've seen some pretty amazing things, with no power drain at all."

"So explain those, then."

Troy shrugged again. "I can't. Not all of them. We do look for explanations while we're on site, you know, and we often find them. Doors that rattle or open in a cross-breeze, air bubbles in the plumbing, warped reflections in old mirrors, sometimes even just people playing pranks. But some of them, we can't explain."

Ben's eyes were pulled to the suitcases and shelves around them. "But they show up on your instruments."

"Usually. Like you said: on a basic level, all of this stuff is designed to recognize different kinds of energy, and express that energy to us. Right?" Troy pulled the photo across the table and looked at it fondly. "Sometimes it just works better than we expected."

Ben stared at him for a long moment, and eventually Troy laughed. "You still don't believe me, do you?"

Aware of thoughtful silence from his inner career coach, Ben answered carefully. "Let's just say... I would like more evidence before I draw any conclusions."

"Well," Troy said, standing, "come to Vermont with us. Maybe you'll find some. I don't care if I have to pay you out of my own pocket. We could use someone like you on our team."

"W-what?" Ben stammered. "Really?" *Try to be more confident.*

"Absolutely. I think you'd be a great addition. But bear in mind, if you do come with us, you'll be swimming against the stream. We're all believers. You don't think ghosts exist? You think it's all hoax photography and rational explanations?" He leaned forward, grinning. "Prove it."

Ben blinked at him, then started to smile. "Maybe I will."

"Good." Troy slapped Ben on the shoulder. "Welcome aboard." He strode out of the room, calling to Rachel and Paolo.

Ben took a deep breath and looked around the room full of sensing equipment and recording devices.

Playground!

On Location

Rachel stood in the living room and turned in a circle, taking in the floor-to-ceiling bookshelves, the gently worn furniture on hardwood floors, and the leafy view of the park. "What's wrong with it?"

"Nothing," the man in the corner blurted. He'd shown up ten minutes late for their appointment, saying, "I'm Murray-the-landlord" as a single word, had rabbited up the stairs to the apartment, and since then, as far as Rachel could tell, had spent his time either watching her closely or further unravelling the cuff of his sweater. "It's perfectly fine. Why do you ask?"

"You said it's been empty for two months, but it's priced better than most places in this neighbourhood and it looks like it's in great shape. Even the furniture seems all right. So what's wrong with it?"

"Nothing! Really."

"I mean, there's always something, right?" Rachel went on cheerfully. "Like an over-sensitive smoke detector, or four screaming kids living upstairs, or leaky plumbing." She wandered around the room, keeping him on the edge of sight. "Dangerous neighbours? Termites? No decent coffee for miles?"

Rachel stopped pacing when his face twitched. She was at the mouth of a short hallway between the living room and the kitchen. Looking around, she saw only an old light fixture above her head and a painting on the wall.

"No, no. There's nothing wrong with it." Murray's words tumbled over themselves. "I mean, I've had applicants. Lots. But something always fell through, that's all. Failed the credit check or whatnot."

"Hmm," Rachel said. A dull ache was uncoiling at the base of her skull. "Okay, well, I've got another apartment to see at –" she checked her watch and chose a time "– one-thirty, so I have to go, but I should be able to let you know one way or the other by about two o'clock. The number I have is your cell phone, right?"

Murray followed her toward the door. "But...wait. Do you want the place or not? I mean, I - I'm busy, I can't just hang around until you decide. Plus you still have to apply, and even then –"

"Oh, go on and do what you have to: I have your phone number. But really, just between us, the application's only a formality, isn't it?" She smiled conspiratorially at him. "Let's keep this simple. If I decide to live here, I'll let you know this afternoon, and then I can move in this weekend. That way we can do a fifteenth-to-fifteenth lease."

"But all the other leases –"

"See, an immediate move-in is good for you here, because then this wouldn't be sitting empty, and you'd know the place is in responsible hands. And I'd get a fantastic place to live. It's win-win, Murray." With a last look around the apartment, Rachel walked out and waited for him on the landing. "And I promise I'll let you know by two o'clock what I've decided, okay? Super! Talk to you later." Waving over her shoulder, she pattered downstairs and out the front door.

As soon as she could, she ducked into the park she had seen from the apartment windows and found a place to stand with a view of the street, watching through the foliage as Murray the landlord climbed into a battered Toyota and drove away. She ate an apple, waiting until the last of her headache subsided, and when he didn't return, she wiped her fingers on her jeans and headed back toward the building.

An elderly man answered her knock at the door of the ground-floor apartment and eyed her warily.

"Hi," Rachel said with a smile. "I'm –"

"I'm not buying anything. And I don't want a new religion."

"Great, me neither. I'm thinking of moving into the apartment upstairs, and I just wanted to talk to the people here to see what the building's like."

"It's fine," he said. "Quiet. We'd like to keep it that way. You a student?" Suspicion sharpened his gaze.

"Nope," she answered cheerfully. "Graduated last week."

"Hmph. Unemployed."

"Not for long, now that I'm a respectable adult like yourself." He looked unconvinced. "No problems I should know about, then? Murray the landlord – he's all right?"

"No worse than others."

"So how come the place above you has been empty for so long? You some kind of tuba-playing troublemaker or something?" She gave her best smile to take the sting out of her words, but his face creased itself into a deeper scowl.

"I got things to do." The door swung shut with a bang.

"Thanks for your time," she called as his footsteps receded. "Nice talking to you." Cranky old man from *Scooby-Doo*, she added silently. Jinkies.

She headed for the stairs.

On the third floor landing, she paused to listen to the noise through the walls. Her knock was answered by a woman in paint-splattered overalls and a haze of salsa music.

"Hi," Rachel said. "Sorry to bother you, but I'm thinking of moving in downstairs, and I'm just trying to get a sense of the building. You know how landlords never really tell you *everything*." She added just the right amount of exasperation.

The woman laughed. "Smart idea."

"Oh? Something I should know?"

"No, no," the other said. "Murray's pretty good about getting something fixed if it goes wrong, mowing lawns, clearing the driveway, that sort of thing. At least he's nearby. And the rent is amazing for this area."

"Yeah, I noticed."

"When we first came, we considered that apartment downstairs first, but then the guy who was living in this one moved out suddenly, and I wanted the extra light for my work." She gestured vaguely at her colour-smeared clothes. "It'd be great if you moved in – we haven't been comfortable with it being empty for so long. It's like inviting a break-in or something, you know?"

"Has that been a problem around here?"

"No, no – I don't want to give you the wrong idea. It's just kind of a strange history. A nice young couple were the most recent ones in there, but they weren't even here half a year. Before them it was some guy, I think he was a mechanic, but he moved out after a few months, too. Before that... oh yes, Mr. Franklin took it when we took this place." She lowered her voice. "You'll probably meet him on moving day, if you take the apartment. He's on the ground floor now, only lasted a few months downstairs. I'm not sure why, though – he's not much for conversation."

Rachel resisted the urge to claim Mr. Franklin as an old familiar friend.

The woman in the doorway shrugged. "We're just starting to wonder why no one stays. We aren't that loud, I promise."

"I believe you." Rachel made a show of looking around. "And there's nothing wrong with the building itself?"

"No. We love it. Great location, nice and quiet, close to everything..."

"Maybe that apartment's just cursed," Rachel said lightly, then watched the woman pick at the paint around her knuckles. "Is it cursed?"

"No, of course not."

Rachel raised her eyebrows.

Flecks of dried cobalt blue drifted to the floor. "It's just... something that couple said. But it's silly. I'm sure it's nothing."

"I don't mind silly. What did they say?"

The woman sighed. "They said they kept hearing things. And misplacing stuff – as in, it wasn't where they'd left it when they needed it later. They said it felt... I don't know, haunted or something." She laughed uncertainly.

"Ah."

"They were nice," the woman added. "But a little strange. In a good way, but still... strange."

"Well, fortunately, *I* am completely normal." Rachel gave the woman the sunny smile that had failed to work with Mr. Franklin, and stuck out her hand. "I'm Rachel, by the way. And I do believe I'm going to be your downstairs neighbour."

⑪

Ten days later, Rachel opened her apartment door and Murray the landlord jerked backwards in surprise.

"Hi," Rachel said as she stepped out and locked the door behind her. "Sorry, I'm on a schedule. Were you looking for me?"

"Um, yeah. I just wanted to see how you were settling in." He hesitated a moment before following her down the stairs. "Didn't take you long."

"Well, I'm efficient that way, and there's not much to move in, with a furnished apartment. I'm really enjoying that green club chair near the window, by the way – nice touch – but I put the old bed down in the basement storage. You're welcome to it if someone else wants it."

"Oh, you brought – okay. But everything else is fine? No problems?"

She stopped on the sidewalk and waited for him to catch up. "Should there be?"

"No, no, of course not." He plucked at his sleeve. Different sweater, same unravelling, Rachel noticed.

"Because you sound like you're expecting problems," she said.

"No, no. Just checking in." He reddened in the brilliance of her smile. "Just... glad everything is working out."

"It sure is. And I'll let you know if I have any questions, but for now I have to get going. I'm off to the Ghost Walk downtown."

He stumbled over the curb. Rachel pretended not to notice. "Ghost Walk?"

"Yep. My friend —" she chose a likely-sounding name — "Carol talked me into it. Apparently it hits all the haunted hot spots. Have you ever done it?"

"No. No, never."

"I'll let you know how it is."

"Okay." He sounded like he was waiting for the punchline.

Rachel waved and left him there.

The past week had been interesting, she reflected as she stared out the bus window. The apartment had certainly lived up to its potential. The library-like living room reminded her of her grandmother's house, with its drifting scents of old paper, wood polish and dust. The kitchen felt familiar, too, but that might've been because it looked just like one of those nostalgic 1950s-style diners, with its black and white tile and chrome-rimmed table and chairs. Her own few pieces of furniture and boxes of miscellany had fit into the leftover spaces as if they belonged there. She'd felt immediately at home.

Plus, of course, there was everything else going on: the noises like garbled whispers just beyond hearing, the shifting furniture, the disappearing-reappearing books and hairbrushes, the headache she developed in the passage between living room and kitchen if she lingered too long.

Pretty much exactly like home, really.

Then again, at home she'd known what to expect, with five generations of lore to support it, and at least three self-proclaimed sensitives at any family gathering, trying to impress her father with the accuracy of their readings. But that was there; here she wasn't sure what was happening. She was starting fresh. New city, new graduate, new grown-up freedom. Maybe it was pride, but she had promised herself she wouldn't call home for help: she'd sort it out herself instead. So here she was, sorting it out.

Rachel pulled the cord and got off the bus in front of an old red stone building with a black clapboard sign on the sidewalk. GHOST WALK STARTS HERE!! *Stories from our haunted city – Tonight 8pm.*

She was a few minutes early, so she hitched herself onto the stair-well's wrought-iron railing and waited, watching as others arrived.

First to appear were three giggling girls in their early twenties. Having so recently been a student herself, Rachel knew immediately they were going to be squealers. Then came an earnest-looking middle-aged couple in windbreakers, clutching maps and notebooks: historian tourists, she decided, with charmingly eccentric interests in the occult. A tall man with impressive shoulders arrived alone and watched the group from a few paces away. He was maybe ten years older than Rachel, and his calm gaze met hers once with a nod. She tentatively pegged him as law enforcement, or maybe military. The last arrivals were a tired-look-ing couple coaxing a teen boy more interested in a game on his phone than anything else. She suspected the parents would pretend to listen to the tour, but mostly were just glad to be out with someone else in charge. Rachel considered the kid and gave even odds whether he'd keep playing his game or become interested and ask a thousand questions.

At eight o'clock exactly, a figure in a black, billowing hooded cape opened the front door of the building and raised an old-fashioned lan-tern aglow with imitation candle light. "Be ye here to learn the terrible dark secrets of this, our fair city?" it hissed in a stage whisper as the group fell silent. "The secrets… of the restless *dead?*"

Oh, dear God, thought Rachel. Without deciding to, she glanced over at the tall man. His face was carefully blank, but he slid his eyes over to hers and raised his brows. He and Rachel smothered identical grins and looked away simultaneously.

"Um, I guess," one of the girls ventured as her friends giggled around her.

"Well, then," the caped figure intoned, drawing the lantern closer and beckoning with a black-nailed finger. "Gather 'round, and we shall begin… And we begin *here!* For *this* was the city's first courthouse, and in the name of rough justice did many poor souls here suffer their last days." The group trooped up the stairs as the figure retreated into the building's dim foyer. "In the miserable cells below our feet, they wasted away on meagre prison rations, waiting for their day in court – only to be sentenced to *hang* from the *neck* until *dead* in the courtyard beyond!"

"Cool," the kid muttered, not looking up from his game.

Rachel looked around at the modern office doors lining the ground floor. The building around her felt unoccupied, cavernous, and not the least bit otherworldly. She sighed.

She might be calling home for help, after all.

⌘

An hour and a half later, the twenty-somethings had each squealed at least twice, the historians had questioned a date in the guide's spiel, the boy had put away his phone and was asking for more gruesome details at each stop, and Rachel was glad the night had settled in, so that her facial expression was mostly hidden from view.

She found herself walking at the back of the group as they moved between sites. The tall man had drifted closer as the night went on, and though he wasn't walking next to her, she felt vaguely as if they were travelling together. She hadn't offered any conversation. If he wanted to speak beyond matching meaningful eyebrows and mutual incredulous glances, he would. In the meantime she'd amused herself by sorting fact from fiction in their guide's commentary, learning more about architecture and history than the secrets of the dead.

Then they straggled into the shadowy halls of a long-disused hospital wing, and all the hairs on the back of Rachel's neck stood up. She slowed her pace and looked around.

Some of the rest of the group seemed affected, too – they were more subdued here, and the boy moved closer to his parents. The tallest giggler faded into silence when her friends didn't respond in kind.

"This," their guide said, with something less than his usual dramatic edge, "is what's left of St. Michael's Hospice."

Tuning him out, Rachel turned slowly in a circle.

This place…

Her father's voice whispered impatiently in her memory. *You've got an ear for the other side, Rachel. Don't ignore it. Pay attention when it calls.*

She was so intent on finding whatever it was that she almost didn't notice when the guide moved on and the group shuffled quietly down the hallway. She lagged behind until a draft raised goosebumps on her arm.

Rachel turned to see the black hollow of a stairwell, agape between pale walls of peeling paint. It sighed more cool air over her as she stared.

"What is it?" a quiet voice nearby asked. She knew without looking that it was the tall man. "Do you see something?"

"Nearly," she breathed, unthinking. "On the landing…" She squinted as a headache stretched across the base of her skull.

The man was beside her now, gazing intently up the stairs. Belatedly she noticed he was holding something about the size of a television remote in his hand. There was just enough light that she could see its back-lit gauge. As its needle twitched, her headache dug its claws in.

"What is that thing?"

"EMF detector," he murmured back, his eyes flickering down to the display. "Confirming what you seem to already know: something's there."

You couldn't tell without it? Rachel wondered, hearing her father's dismissive snort in her head, but she said nothing as she kept her eyes on the stairwell. For a dream-like instant, she saw –

"Hey, you two!" a harried shout echoed down the hall. "Keep up – we're moving on!" The guide's voice had lost all its staged mystery.

"*Idiot,*" the tall man growled, and Rachel couldn't help but grin at the depth of his irritation.

"It's okay," she said, and nodded toward the stairwell. It was just an empty slice of darkness now, and her headache was fading. "We'll just have to come back."

He glanced over at her as they headed toward the group. "Will we?"

"Yeah. Unless you have a problem with breaking and entering?"

He considered this. "Maybe we could ask permission first. See how that goes."

She shrugged. "Whatever floats your boat."

He let out a startled laugh as they rejoined the group. "I'm Troy, by the way," he whispered as everyone shuffled forward again.

"Rachel," she murmured back. "You want to go for coffee after this debacle is over?"

"Uh…"

"And no, I'm not flirting. You are very much not my type." She ignored the relief that crossed his face. "I just have a feeling we could maybe help each other."

"Well, then." He gave her a thoughtful glance as the group jostled out a side door and into the cold night air. "Maybe this won't have been a waste of time after all."

☊

That weekend, Troy left his wet shoes on the doormat, hung his dripping coat on the doorknob, and dropped his damp duffel bag beside them. He followed Rachel into the living room in sock feet. "Nice place," he said.

"Thanks. It's even nicer when the sun's shining, but who wants to look for ghosts then? Boring. You want a coffee or something?"

He padded after her, down the short hall. She could feel him looking around the apartment as they went. "You said it was furnished when you moved in?"

"Yep, so unfortunately I can't take credit for this amazing kitchen." She gestured and pretended his polite interest was more enthusiastic. "I know, right? I always feel like I should bake cookies and wait for Wally and the Beav to come home. But if you were thinking haunted artifact, it does leave a lot of possibilities."

"Yes, it does."

"Which is why one of the first things I did was a smudging cleanse – sweetgrass, sage and a few other things the indigenous people in this area used ceremonially, just in case this place was built on significant ground. I had one of my professors come in to help me, and she said she couldn't feel anything in particular." She sighed. "So then I went to the city archives and pulled the records of the land and ownership as far back as I could find. One family had it for generations through the 1800s, and then about eighty years ago it was bought by Jewish family, so I asked one of last year's TAs to find me some protective prayers in the Shulhan 'Aruk. He can get me a mezuzah, but I think that'll be a last resort. I mean, I did well in the class, but it's not as if I'm actually Jewish and practicing daily, so any of its power would be pretty diluted, I think." Rachel looked up from the coffeemaker to find Troy staring at her. "What?"

"You… what do you mean, in the class?"

"Comparative religions. Well, that's my degree. I think that particular class was Mystical Traditions in Contemporary Judeo-Christian Practice – something like that. But I've just graduated, which means I'm stuffed full of knowledge and have a whole pile of resources at my fingertips." She waggled all ten fingers at him and he seemed to snap out of his startlement. "I just have to figure out what's calling to me." At his blank look, she amended, "Figure out what the situation demands."

"Okay." He nodded, then nodded again as if collecting his thoughts. "Okay. So you did all that, but I gather nothing's changed."

"Nope."

"So… it might still be a spirit attached to something in the apartment. The furniture isn't yours, so that was here. What else?"

"Some of the books on the shelves in the living room aren't mine, but they fill space and make me look literary, so I left them. And some of the larger paintings I didn't hate, so they're still here. Plus a couple of them are screwed into the wall for some reason, and I couldn't be bothered to find the right screwdriver." She took two mugs from the cupboard. "Oh, and most of the dishes were here, but I don't think I've ever heard of a haunted colander before."

Troy frowned. "The paintings are screwed into the walls?"

She nodded, pouring coffee into the mugs. "It's weird, I know. I've thought of three possibilities: one, to prevent some crazed art fan stealing them; two, to cover giant holes Murray the landlord couldn't fix properly; three, to protect them from being thrown around when the spook is feeling feisty."

"Do things get thrown around?"

"Not that I've seen or heard, but I've only been here two weeks. Things do wander from where they were put, though, and fall off tables and such."

"Hmm." Troy leaned against the kitchen counter, Rachel against the table, and they drank their coffee in silence, watching the rain slide down the kitchen window. "And you said... voices? Plus your headaches," Troy said after a moment.

Rachel took a moment to be grateful for his tone: politely curious, without a trace of disbelief or mockery. Growing up, it hadn't taken her long to realize that, while her family might live comfortably among furtive noises and darting shadows, her friends from school didn't. In fact, most of the people everywhere else didn't. She'd long since outgrown denying her heritage, but she'd also learned that, when she was out in the world, it was easier to deafen what her father called her "ear". Though lately the headaches had made that harder.

She hadn't told her father about those yet. She suspected he'd be delighted.

She waved away the sudden wisp of homesickness and focused on Troy. He was large enough to nearly overwhelm the little kitchen, but his sock feet were endearing, and he radiated calm attention. After the ghost walk, they'd found the nearest coffee shop and talked until the staff closed the place down at midnight. Then he'd waited with her for a cab and promised to help if she got in touch. She'd felt simultaneously safe with and comforted by him. Maybe he was using some sort of law enforcement empathy training on her? She hadn't gotten around to asking about his background...

"Rachel?"

"Right – yes, voices. Not loud, only whispers, just barely there, like hearing a low television through a wall. And yes, I've looked into that: it's not a television through a wall," she added before he could speak.

He nodded again. "They sound garbled, almost – I can't make out any words. And they happen anytime, day and night. There doesn't seem to be a pattern."

"And the headaches?"

"Worst in the hall, but they do sometimes flare up elsewhere." She made a face. "I just don't think they should be on our list of evidence."

"Why not? From what you said, when it happened on the walk it seemed to corroborate the EMF spike on the detector. I know that's only one example, but I gather it's happened before." When she nodded, he went on. "So if you're responding to a spirit's energy –"

"But how do we know it's a spirit I'm reacting to? The world's full of electromagnetic energy, more every day. I'll have the damn headaches for the rest of my life." Just like my great-aunt did, she thought, but went on, trying to sound reasonable. "All we *might* be able to prove is that I can confirm a change in an EM field. Not that it's tied to a spirit."

He thought a moment. "I get it. Like getting food poisoning after a big meal and not being sure which food caused it."

"Well, that's disgusting. Thank you for that."

"You know, we could probably figure out some sort of testing series to –"

She held up a hand. "Not until I can stop thinking about food poisoning."

Grinning, Troy pushed away from the counter. "Okay. I've brought all the equipment I could carry. Where do you want to begin?"

"Living room's got the double whammy," she said, leading the way. "Whispers plus stuff moving."

As Troy paced silently and patiently across the living room for the third time, studying the readout on his EMF meter, Rachel thought, It's not as if I need it to be haunted. I'm not some homesick schoolgirl. There could be all sorts of explanations. But if he doesn't find anything, should I be relieved or embarrassed?

Before she could decide, she noticed his expression change. "Something?"

"Maybe. The room's at about point-seven-five milligauss – that's pretty standard, and of course it's higher near your television and stereo. No surprises until we come over here." He waved her toward the window and her favourite reading spot, with its green club chair and spindly side table. Troy swept the meter in front of both and she watched the needle shiver. "It doesn't register much of a change, but it's hard to see why a chair and a wooden table would register at all."

"Well, if it helps, I'm pretty sure this table moves when I'm not looking. And it will sometimes shed whatever I leave on it."

Troy studied it. "Move how? Shed how?"

"It scoots over a few inches, toward the window or away. But it's so flimsy I could almost believe I just brushed it out of place without noticing when I got up from the chair."

Troy poked one corner with a finger and made a face when the whole table slid away. Rachel shrugged.

"So whatever you leave on it just falls onto the ground?" he asked.

"Sometimes yes, so then it's lying nearby. Easy. But sometimes it ends up across the room instead."

"As in… fell off the table and rolled away? It's an older building. How level is the floor?" He moved toward his equipment bag again.

"I don't know. How level does it need to be for, say, a book to fall off the table and end up on the third shelf over there by the door?" His startled expression made her feel vaguely triumphant. This place doesn't need to be haunted, she reminded herself. New life out in the world, remember?

Shaking his head, Troy placed a carpenter's level on the ground in the center of the room, studied it, and turned it ninety degrees. He came back to the table and chair and repeated the process. "Not perfectly level, but not enough of a slope to roll very far." He sat back on his heels and considered the bookshelf. "Or vertically."

"So now what?"

"I haven't heard any of the whispers you've mentioned. Have you, while we've been doing this?" She shook her head, so he stood up. "Let's see if the voice recorder has caught anything we didn't."

They stood in the gray, watery light from the window and listened to their voices, tinny and overloud, from the speakers. Rachel couldn't hear anything special, but at one point Troy rewound a piece and held the speaker right to his ear. Then he shook his head. "No. For a moment, I thought I heard something, but…"

"Okay." She suppressed a sigh. "So is this room a bust?"

"I'll reset this recorder and we'll leave it here. We'll set up the second one in the next room."

They repeated the whole process in the bedroom with even fewer results. Troy remained his patient, pleasant self as they took standard readings and listened to unremarkable audio files. Rachel wiped a wrinkle off the bedspread and told herself she was not disappointed. "Thank goodness," she said aloud. "Who wants a haunted bedroom? Total cliché. Let's do the hallway next. Maybe we can figure out the headache thing, at least."

It's in your blood, her father's voice murmured in her mind. She ignored it.

In the narrow confines of the little hallway, Troy had barely enough room to hold the EMF reader in front of him and turn in a circle. Next to him, Rachel rubbed the base of her skull and resisted the urge to flee to the kitchen.

"Ah," he said, as the needle lurched and settled. "There's one problem confirmed, at least: we've jumped from point seven-five everywhere else to about four milligauss here. No wonder you can feel it." He held the meter above his head, toward the light fixture, and the needle quivered again. "Probably the wiring in this old thing."

"Faulty wiring," Rachel said, staring at the fixture until purple spots flared across her vision. "That's a relief."

"Until it burns the place down." Troy murmured. He offered an encouraging smile and she had the sense that she wasn't hiding her disappointment as well as she thought. "Your landlord should probably get this looked at." He started to lower the meter, then frowned as the needle jumped again.

Rachel watched him wave the meter in front of him once more, then move it closer to the wall. "Why is it stronger there? Oh my God – is it reacting to that painting? Do I have a haunted artifact?"

"You have... something," Troy said. "Oh. It's one of the screwed-in ones." He looked sideways at her. "It's time to find the right kind of screwdriver. Phillips head, number two. I should have one in the equipment bag."

"On it." She squeezed past him and returned with a pair of screwdrivers. "I don't know why you have so many doubles of things in there, but this way we can each do one side." She attacked the top corner with an excitement she didn't try to hide, and pretended she couldn't see, out of the corner of her eye, him smiling again.

When the last screw was out and Troy lifted the painting off the wall, he immediately turned it over, squinting at the back of the canvas. "The framer's label is on here, but it doesn't –"

"I don't think it's the painting," Rachel said. "I think it's probably this."

He looked up as she touched the edges of the neat three-inch hole in the wall. She tapped a fingernail on the silvery device standing like a futuristic flower behind the wall's surface. "Please tell me this isn't a camera." She was pleased with how calm she sounded.

"No," Troy said. "It looks like a microphone. Or a speaker? They're starting to look the same these days. Can you move it at all? Pull it out?"

Rachel wedged two fingers into the hole and tugged on the wire stem. It moved, but she pulled it toward them only a little before meeting resistance. "It's caught on something or attached at the other end, wherever that is. Not in this apartment, I'm guessing." She glared at it. "So now what?"

"Well. For your own peace of mind, I would suggest we check for others. Then we figure out where they lead and who put them there." Troy's voice was angrier than hers had been. She appreciated that.

"Figure out how?" Rachel asked as they returned to the living room. "Use the EMF meter again?"

"I'm not sure it's sensitive enough to track something like that to a remote source. But it might explain…" He moved directly to the window with its reading chair and table, watching the needle wave again. He lowered himself to the floor as Rachel joined him. "I don't think it's the chair. The upholstery looks intact and someone might feel it when they sat down."

"The table's too old and spindly to have anything like that in it."

"Agreed. Which leaves…" He moved over to the radiator under the window and peered through the narrow vent slots. "I need a flashlight." Rachel started to stand, but he hauled himself upright and waved her down. "You went last time, and I might want a few other things."

Rachel sat and stared accusingly at the radiator. "Murray the landlord," she murmured. "You little weasel. Faking a haunt to scare away tenants? Is that any way to run a business?" Then she noticed the EMF meter, lying near the table where Troy had pushed it aside. It wasn't facing the radiator anymore, but its needle was still quivering above normal. Frowning, she pushed it closer to the table and watched the needle move again. Sighing, she upended the table with a single annoyed push. It clattered to the floor just as Troy returned.

He paused. "Problem?"

"We'll see."

"Okay. Uh, do you mind if I take the front of this radiator off? I think it'll make things easier."

"Knock yourself out." Rachel hauled the table into her lap. The underside of the table was plain unfinished wood with dustwebs in the joints and blackened nails holding everything together. The legs were slender, but seemed solid when she knocked on them. She ran her fingers down their sides again.

There was a hollow metallic *chuh-clunk* as the radiator casing separated from the wall. Troy hoisted it out of the way and straightened. "Son of a bitch."

Two more silvery devices were glinting at her from between the radiator guts. Their wires hugged the wall and disappeared into neat holes drilled in the floor.

"They must be speakers," Troy said grimly. "I doubt microphones would get any clear audio next to all this and behind a metal grille."

"I'm not sure I feel relieved about that." Rachel frowned at the speakers, then down at the table feet in her lap, lifting them into the light. "In related news: do these look like magnets to you?"

Troy stared at them. He picked up one of the long screws he'd loosened from the radiator casing and tossed it toward her. She fumbled the catch, but it bounced up to the end of the table leg and stuck there as if glued. Troy's frown deepened. "Pretty powerful ones."

"You have got to be kidding me." Rachel looked over, pleased to see him still looking so angry. "You know what? You should come meet my neighbour. It'll be fun."

⟨⊞⟩

"Hi, Mr. Franklin," Rachel said cheerfully. "Can I borrow your broom?"

"What?" He scowled at her, then up at Troy, looming over her shoulder.

"Your broom. Can I borrow it? I don't have one yet."

"Can't be borrowing my stuff all the time," the old man grumbled.

"This is the first time I've ever done it."

"Still." He eyed Troy again and shuffled away from the door, half-closing it defensively. "Just… wait here. I'll bring it."

They waited until his footsteps receded, then Troy stretched his arm over Rachel's head and used a single finger to push the door open as far as it could go. They peered into the apartment beyond.

"Can you see anything?" she whispered.

"No. Too dark back there."

Mr. Franklin rounded the corner, fumbling with the head of an old push-broom. He looked up and froze when he saw them in the open doorway.

"Oh, that's okay," Rachel smiled. "You don't have to take the magnets out. I'll just use it as is, and stay away from that little table." She held out a hand.

Franklin looked at her, then at Troy, then at the broom. His rounded shoulders sagged further. "Aw, hell."

Troy crossed his arms. "Mr. Franklin. I believe you owe this young lady an explanation."

"What do you care?" the old man demanded. He absently handed Rachel the broom when she waggled her hand for it. "You don't live here. Who are you, anyway?"

"Her colleague," Troy said, a fraction of a second after Rachel said, "My housekeeper." She examined the head of the push broom and showed it to Troy. "Look: magnets." She raised the wide edge of the brush to the ceiling and dragged it along. "Stand in the right place, and presto. Spooky moving table. Wonder what else it works on?"

"And the disembodied voices from hidden speakers?" Troy asked.

"Yeah," Rachel mused. "What is that? It's quiet, but it barely even sounds like English. It's very unsettling."

"Mostly Irish Gaelic," Franklin said. "My wife's old language tapes."

She blinked at him. "And you set up those speakers all on your own before you left? That's a lot of work."

"And know-how," Troy added.

"I haven't been this old forever," Franklin snapped. "I had a career once, and a certain amount of intelligence. I used them."

"So you've chased away two tenants before me, and poor Murray's about to have a nervous breakdown. For what? Why bother?" She handed back the broom, and the man knocked the pole end on the floor a few times, twisting his mouth this way and that in annoyance.

"I loved that apartment," he said suddenly, as if a dam had burst. "Loved all the books and the view of the park. And that green chair by the window. But then the doc said my damn knees couldn't take the stairs anymore. Not every day. I held out as long as I could, but it's not like Murray's going to put in an elevator, and where would he put it, anyway? This isn't some big highrise yuppie condo in the city. So I moved out. Down to this dingy little hole. Might as well live in the basement. Look at the light in here, just look at it! It's like this even when it isn't raining." He glowered over his shoulder.

"So before you left…?" Troy prompted.

He turned back to them with a sigh. "Figured if I could keep other people out, it'd at least be quieter in here. Wouldn't have to listen to people traipsing around all day overhead, enjoying the view and the chair. Thought maybe if it was empty I could get in there once in a while for an afternoon of peace and quiet. But that moron Murray changed the locks after each person moved out." He scowled at Murray in absentia.

"So he doesn't know you've been doing this?"

Franklin made a rude noise. "But I suppose you'll tell him." He eyed Rachel with his usual suspicious belligerence, but now she saw fear behind it.

She thought about the convenient neighbourhood, low rent, and creaky old knees. Then she thought of something else.

"Murray changed the locks every time," she said. "Which means you haven't been inside the apartment lately? To move stuff around?"

"Not from inside," the old man said, pushing the magnet-laden broom across the floor dejectedly. "Haven't been up there in months."

Rachel beamed. "Well, I'll have to invite you up for a drink or something sometime. After you take back all your little toys, of course, because they creep me out. Oh, and you'll have to promise not to do anything like that again while I'm there. You're messing up our data."

His wary eyes searched her face, then moved to Troy. "Your what?"

"Promise," Rachel said sternly.

After a moment, he jerked his head in a wary nod. "Fine. I promise. Don't damage those speaker wires when you're pulling them out. I'll disconnect them from here and they should haul up just fine."

"Great. Well, Mr. Franklin, this has been very educational. You have a good day, now."

Standing in bewildered silence, Franklin watched them climb the first few stairs. Then he eased his door shut with a quiet click.

A moment later, Troy murmured under his breath, "I would've gotten away with it, too, if it weren't for you meddling kids!"

Rachel stopped and turned to look at him.

He shrugged. "Sorry, I couldn't resist. He was just so –"

"I know!" Rachel interrupted gleefully. "Oh, I was right. Troy, you and I are going to get along just fine. Famously, even."

"Or you and my son will. He loves Scooby-Doo."

"Promise me something, though," Rachel said as she stepped inside the apartment and surveyed the remnants of their investigation. "Don't ever tell my father that we used all these... gadgets. He's open-minded about a lot of things, but this?" She picked the EMF meter off the shelf in example. "I'd never hear the end of it."

"Okay," Troy said, "though I sense an interesting story behind that request."

"Ha: generations of them. Maybe I'll even tell them, someday. They might just pop up, now that we're going to be working together."

"Are we?" He sounded more amused than surprised.

"Sure. Like you said downstairs: colleagues."

"And you said 'housekeeper.'"

"That was a joke, because of the broom. Jeesh. You'll have to keep up, Troy, if you want to work with me. Besides, I don't need a housekeeper – stuff I leave over there by the window ends up right here, neat and tidy on the third shelf by the door." She held up the EMF meter again, grinning expectantly.

Troy looked at the overturned table, the exposed radiator, and the jumble of debris by the window that now did not include the EMF meter. He looked at the device in her hand. Then he considered the door she'd just unlocked and the empty, silent apartment around them.

Outside, thunder rumbled and lightning flashed.

"Jinkies," he said, and Rachel laughed in delight.

Alternate Ending

Shipboard – Five days out

Troy was woken by the clang of a hatch swinging shut, sound and impact reverberating through the bulkhead beside his bunk. Conversation rose and fell past his room, underscored by heavy footfalls that made the deck plates tremble. Apparently at least some of the day shift was on its way to the mess hall for breakfast. Troy couldn't smell any food, though, only glossy paint over steel. He should have been used to that oily scent after two years spent mostly on board – and he was – but it went right to his gut first thing every morning, dulling his appetite.

He rolled his head over the pillow, blinking at the empty bunk across the room and letting out a slow, even breath.

Maybe Alex would be awake when he visited. Maybe today would be a good day.

(ft)

"Sir."

"Sir."

"Morning, sir."

Of course Darijo would be the one to add a greeting to the acknowledgement.

"Morning, gents." Troy gave all three a smile as they passed, but if his nod was mostly aimed at Darijo, the other two would be fine with that. He was trying not to scare them off. They weren't "religious", or at least that's what they had said early on, trying to explain without offense why they were so awkward around him. Troy had tried to tell them that he'd found his chaplain role to be more of a counselor and morale monitor than a hellfire-and-brimstone spokesman for any established creed, but they were too new to the life, too new to this ship. Whatever their childhood church baggage, it hadn't yet been unpacked into practical Navy footlockers of experience. So they kept their eyes on his lieutenant stripes instead of the crosses on his collar tabs and watched him sideways, as if he'd break into psalm or sermon without warning.

The three trooped on, leaving Troy to stand a moment and consider his next move. This was a stalling tactic, because he knew where he was going. He turned and nearly knocked down someone just leaving the dining hall.

"Sorry about that, Commander," Troy said, once they'd extricated themselves. "Maybe you should make more noise as you go. Everyone else clomps and echoes like stormtroopers."

"We're all wearing rubber-soled boots," the commander pointed out. "We should be able to walk silently anywhere. Not my fault if you lummox-sized types can't manage it."

"We're Navy, not ninjas."

She shook her head, but she was wearing her rare, fractional smile. "Maybe you're just not making the effort, Lieutenant. I'd write you up for it, but I guess it's too late now. You getting yourself all squared away?"

Troy felt his own smile sag a little. "Yes, ma'am. Just a few more papers to sign."

"We do love our paperwork. And we'll miss you around here, Lieutenant. Are you daydreaming of civilian life already?" When he blinked in confusion, she nodded at the dining room behind them. "I walked in right behind you and ate at the next table over, but you weren't noticing much. Now you're packing a snack for later?" She eyed a napkin-wrapped bagel in his hand.

"It's not for me. I thought I'd go see Lightner this morning."

Her expression stilled. "Ah." After a short silence, she said, "They do feed him in there, you know."

"Yes, ma'am." Under the pressure of her waiting gaze he offered something close to truth. "Peace offering."

Her eyebrow quirked in query.

"I'm hoping maybe it brings him some."

She looked at him a moment longer, expression still fixed. "Like I said: we'll miss you around here. Good luck with him." She turned on her heel and strode away, almost silent on the metal decking.

You could visit him too, Troy wanted to say. Sighing, he headed toward the infirmary.

⚓

"Sir? What are you doing here? Oh, God, you're not here to give me last rites, are you?"

Troy had the sense Seaman Andrew Bonneville was only half joking. "Not that I know of – I didn't even know you were here. Do you think you need last rites?"

Bonneville pulled himself taller on his mattress. "No, sir. Nope, not at all. I'm only here for observation. I swear, I'm really not worth anyone's time. Maybe you could convince D to let me go early? Sir?" He radiated hopeful optimism.

"Son, I'm afraid even my word wouldn't be good enough for our med tech. I'm not the one to get you out of here any faster."

"He's right," called Darijo's voice from the tiny office walled off in the corner. "So stop complaining, Bonny."

Troy smiled sympathetically. "What happened?"

"Nothing, sir." The kid fiddled with his bedsheet. "Stupid accident, that's all."

"Possible concussion, is all," Darijo corrected him, appearing at Troy's side. "Knocked himself senseless during an emergency drill

97

yesterday, then heaved up his lunch all over my nice clean infirmary. So you, Seaman Bonneville, will be here under observation until I say otherwise." Darijo turned to Troy and looked at the bagel in his hand. "We do feed our patients, you know."

"I know."

Darijo's knowing gaze travelled from the bagel to Troy's face, probably assessing heart rate, blood pressure, distraction and God knew what else besides. "All right, then." He nodded toward the far corner of the room. "Not sure how he'll be for you. He wasn't very responsive when I arrived, and Dr. Monro told me he didn't have a very good night."

Troy maintained his chaplain face while his insides shrank around his breakfast. "Thanks."

Darijo nodded and moved away.

"You're here to see the lieutenant-commander, sir?" Bonneville's voice was a whisper, though Lightner probably couldn't hear from this distance. Sometimes he didn't even hear you when you were next to him, Troy reflected, but maybe Bonneville didn't know that.

"That's the plan."

Bonneville glanced toward the other end of the room with a frown that didn't sit well on his amiable face. "Hopefully he's better than last night. I mean, my bunkmate snores like a sawmill – I figure if I can sleep through that, I can sleep through anything. But…" Bonneville trailed off. He looked up, a worried crease between his eyebrows. "Do you think you can help him, sir?"

"I hope so," Troy said. "Do you have everything you need? I would've brought you a bagel, too, if I'd known you'd be here."

Bonneville's smile was a shadow of its usual self. "Thanks, sir, but I'm all right. You get that to Lieutenant-Commander Lightner, see if he'll eat it. Maybe it'll do him some good."

Troy headed toward the far corner and let his own smile fade. *I could use some help here,* he thought, touching the cross on his collar tab. *I know it's not a fiery furnace or a lion's den, but I'm running out of time and I don't seem to be accomplishing much alone…*

He slowed his approach as he rounded the corner of the cot. "Lightner?" The huddled form under the crisp white sheets didn't stir. "Alex? It's Troy."

He thought he heard an inhalation.

"Alex?" Troy moved closer. "Are you awake?"

A sudden thrashing motion revealed a face: eyes staring and red-rimmed, angry wounds mauling the left side from crown to cheek, suture punctures just starting to scab over. Close-shorn stubble glittered like ice across the battered scalp and jaw.

"Troy?" Lightner's voice was all gravel. The wrongness of it scraped across Troy's ears.

"Alex." He clasped the hand that drifted upward, and squeezed gently. *Thank you, God.* "Glad to see you awake this time."

"This time?" Lightner's gaze skidded across the room. "How long... have I been...?"

With his free hand, Troy pulled a chair closer, and Lightner's shaky grip fell away at the noise. "About ten days," Troy said as casually as he could. "But it's done you good. How do you feel?"

Those unsettled eyes flared and narrowed.

"I brought you a snack," Troy said after a moment. "I know Darijo and the others take good care of you, but no one likes hospital food, right?"

Lightner froze at the sight of the bagel. Then he slowly pushed the sheets down and inched himself upright against the pillow. Straightened his shirt collar. Ran an unsteady hand over his scalp, yanking it away when his fingers found the wounds.

"Here, buddy. Get that in you." Troy handed over the bagel. "You know what I bet you don't miss, being in here? Coleman, still trying to get the breakfast omelet right. He tried it again yesterday and it was basically a train wreck on a plate. I'm not sure what the problem is, whether it's the ingredients, or him, or what." He rambled on, looking around the room, watching Lightner in his periphery. The man relaxed a little more with each slow bite, so Troy continued his monologue of fluff. He caught Bonneville's eye and got an encouraging thumbs-up.

"Where's Proctor?" Lightner broke in abruptly. "Here?"

Troy's tension came rushing back. "No. Proctor's not here. How about – "

"Where is she?" Lightner was struggling to lift himself from the mattress. "Where is she?"

"Don't move, Alex, just take it easy –"

"Is she safe?" His voice cracked and tumbled. "Did she die? Is she *dead?*"

"No," Darijo said firmly as he stepped up to the bed. "No, sir, she is not dead."

His certainty seemed to hold Lightner in place. "She's not?"

"No, sir." The med tech moved around Troy, stopping at the head of the bed with a glance at the vital sign readouts. "You should lie back, sir. Your head is still healing and too much movement will aggravate it."

"Proctor. She's not here?"

"No, sir." Darijo put a hand on Lightner's shoulder and pushed him gently backwards as he spoke. "Petty Officer Proctor was only here a few hours. She needed more specialized care than we could provide." His tone was matter-of-fact. "We med-evac'd her to the nearest hospital ashore. They've got a full burn unit and first-class rehab folks."

"Burn?" Lightner's face twisted in confusion. "No. Not burned. There was –" He squinted at Troy. "Was a boat. They were – they hid –" Bewilderment edged his voice higher.

Darijo, watching the vitals climb, turned away to tear open a syringe packet.

"Alex," Troy said, taking his cue from Darijo's calm. "Alex. Look at me. Yes, there was a boat. We stopped it for suspected piracy. You led the boarding party for the search. But you were ambushed. Everyone got out – you hear me? But PO Proctor was injured –"

"Boiler room," Lightner said suddenly. "With machetes." His hand crept upward again. "Not fire. Her arm." He seized Darijo's sleeve. "Her arm!"

"Yes, sir. We had to take it off below the elbow," the med tech said, injecting something into the intravenous drip. "But she is alive. She'll start rehab as soon as she's able."

"The fire started afterwards," Troy said. "Best we can figure, it was rigged like a booby trap. One of the pirates set it off as the squad was getting you and Proctor out."

Memory surfaced and sank again behind Lightner's eyes. "Everyone got out. All of us?"

"Everyone," Troy said firmly.

"And Proctor is… not here." His expression eased, but he sounded uncertain.

"Safe, and not here," Darijo confirmed. "Once you're both feeling better, sir, we'll set up a call and you can talk to her yourself." He nodded at Troy and headed back into the ward.

Lightner exhaled, easing back into his pillows. He sat for a few minutes in motionless silence, then rasped, "Thanks. For this – real food."

"Anytime. I could try to bring two next time if you want."

Beyond a twist of his lips, Lightner didn't react. Silence returned.

"Maybe I should let you get some more rest," Troy said.

"Rest. Ha," the other muttered, his eyes half-closed. "You… you're trying to make me stay here. You just want… quarters all to yourself."

Troy smiled in relief. "That's not true. Though I am using your bunk for boot storage. It's been a handy surface for shining and polishing and whatnot."

A breath of a laugh before the crease between his brows reappeared. "Ten days here. You have… how much longer?"

Troy hesitated. "Five days. But don't worry: I'll come in every day until then. You'll be sick of me. You'll be first in line to say farewell and push me off that gangplank."

"Unless they kick me off, too," Lightner murmured. "No good like this." His hand twitched off the sheet just enough to gesture at himself. The scarred side of his face quivered. "Not like…"

"Hey," Troy said firmly. He moved forward until he caught Lightner's gaze and held it. "You are not a lost cause, Alex. Listen. You're damn right I'm trying to keep you here: you need to rest up and heal. So let us help you do that."

After a long moment, Lightner's mouth twitched again. "You ain't the boss of me. Plus. You're chaplain. Shouldn't swear."

"I've got special swearing dispensation, for dealing with stubborn guys like you."

Another breath of a laugh, and they sat in more comfortable silence. When the other man's breathing deepened, Troy silently returned the chair to its original position, whispering, "I'll see you later, Alex."

"Hey," Lightner said. *"Hey."*

Troy turned to find his friend's eyes struggling to open, glazed with sedatives.

"She's not here?" When Troy shook his head, Lightner seemed to grope for words. "But who... who was here?"

"Just me. And your doctors, and Darijo. A few other patients."

"Not now. Then. Then, in the dark. I saw... "

"She hasn't been here, Alex. But she is safe."

"Safe... but. When I woke... she was..." His forehead still creased with effort, his eyelids closed and the murmur wound down.

Troy watched for a moment longer, but Alex Lightner was asleep.

That night, Troy was about to climb into his bunk when someone knocked on his door. When he opened it, he needed a moment to recognize Darijo. The medic's face was grey and somehow adrift, his usual confidence gone.

Troy tensed. "Alex –"

"He's fine." Darijo's head twitched toward the sound of boots echoing down the passageway. "Can I come in?"

"Sure." He flicked the lights back on as Darijo stepped in and stopped in the centre of the room. "You look like you need to sit down."

The med tech's eyes darted toward Lightner's bunk. "I'll stand. I need to…" He took two more steps and turned around. "Something."

Troy sat on the edge of the desk. "What happened?"

Darijo took a deep breath. "Proctor. She didn't make it."

For a long moment, they just stared at each other. Part of Troy thought it was ludicrous their expressions matched so closely in shock and bewilderment. Surely Darijo should be used to this sort of thing.

"What? How?"

"Mersa," Darijo growled, and saw Troy's confusion. Anger sharpened his tone as he started to pace. "MRSA. It's a superbug: an antibiotic-resistant bacterium. It's fast-moving and it's a bitch to get rid of. Shouldn't even happen in the first place." His jaw worked for a moment in silence. "The hospital had an outbreak a couple of days after she arrived. They were dealing with it in-house, trying to keep it quiet so the press wouldn't get hold of it and start a panic. They cut back on visitor hours with some bullshit cover story about the flu, didn't tell the truth to anyone who didn't need to know." In a burst of movement that didn't even break his stride, he kicked the wastebasket across the room. "Apparently we didn't need to know."

"I'm sorry," Troy said quietly, to no response. He watched Darijo pace in another frustrated circle. "So how did we find out?"

The tech completed half a circuit before answering. "This afternoon, Lightner woke up and was asking about her again. I thought a phone call might be good for both of them, so at the end of my shift I called the hospital for an update, hoping to maybe talk to her primary and get an estimate of when Proctor might be up for it. The staff tried to stonewall me, but I kept at it. Eventually they told me." He exhaled. "She died early this morning. Around two a.m."

It was usually the chaplain's task to notify next of kin, and Troy's mind was already surging ahead. Would the hospital release details to him? Had they already called the family? Surely they had; it had been almost a day… He realized Darijo's pacing had stopped. "What? Something else?"

"Lightner." The med tech shook his head. "He keeps insisting he saw her. That he woke up and saw her in the room." He raised his hands as if fending off a protest. "He's had a severe head injury and significant trauma. He's been mostly unconscious for days. He's on meds."

Troy waited, watching the silent struggle on Darijo's face.

"But he was more lucid this afternoon, better than he was with you. Remembered details of the mission and what happened, which is a good sign after injuries like his. But still he… he is sure he saw her last night. Swears it."

Troy considered this. "You said he'd had a bad night."

"Yeah, so I checked the chart notes. He woke up shouting, warning her, telling her to get clear, as if he were reliving it. Not unusual. But it was all directed at the same corner of the ward, and Monro wrote that Lightner's eyes were normal, focused, staring at that corner as if she were right there in the room." Darijo took a deep breath. "Right around two a.m."

This time the silence was complete.

"And so… you think –"

"I think severe head injury, major trauma. Sedatives. Painkillers. But Bonneville was there, too, and he was weird about it this morning. And now…" Darijo rubbed his hand roughly over his face. "Finding this out is a hell of a way to end a day. Sorry. I'm going to go. I just… had to tell someone." The medic had his hand on the door when Troy's voice stopped him.

"Do *you* think he saw her?"

Darijo's shoulders sagged. "I don't know," he said. "My job is physical stuff: fractures and concussions and keeping people breathing. Beyond that – if there is anything beyond that –" He offered a grimacing twist of a smile as he opened the door. "Seems like that's more your department."

Shipboard – Four days out

"Sir?" Bonneville slowed, squinting at him. "What are you doing here? I mean –"

Troy smiled reassuringly, gesturing for the seaman's comrades to go ahead without him. "Could I have a minute?"

"Um. Yes, sir. Of course." He shuffled sideways and propped his gear along the bulkhead, straightening to face Troy like a kid at the principal's office.

"You're not in trouble, Seaman. I just wanted to ask you about the night you were in the infirmary with Lieutenant-Commander Lightner."

Bonneville's eyes slid to the doorway his crewmates had just passed through. Their voices drifted out to fill his moment of hesitation. "What about it, sir?"

"You told me he'd had a bad night. What did you mean by that?"

"Oh. Just that he was pretty restless. He wasn't exactly awake, but he wasn't sleeping soundly, either. He was mumbling a lot. Calling out sometimes."

"It must've been pretty loud, to wake you. Especially given what you said about your bunkmate."

"Well, Doc Monro kept waking me up to make sure I wasn't concussed, so I wasn't getting the best night's sleep either. And it wasn't that he was loud, exactly." Bonneville's voice lowered. "It was more the tone that woke me, sir, if that makes sense. He sounded so... frantic. I'd wake up each time like a shot, thinking it was an emergency for real, that he was in trouble. He was – it was hard to listen to, sir." He cast another glance at the doorway beside them.

"Seaman, if you're worried your friends might find out that you have a compassionate side," Troy said quietly, "I'd be happy to have a chat with them about that."

Bonneville reddened behind his freckles. "Please don't, sir. We heard about PO Proctor at breakfast, and now half of them think I'm as crazy as…" He trailed off, reddening further.

"Alex Lightner is *not* –" A sudden realization drained Troy's outrage. "You saw him calling out to her, didn't you?" The young man's stricken face was his answer. "Bonneville, did you see what he saw?"

"No, sir." But he wouldn't meet Troy's eyes.

"Seaman –"

"No! Sir, there was nothing to see. It was nothing. I checked it the next day and it's just an empty corner."

"You checked it?"

Bonneville ducked his head and stepped back. "I have to report to duty, sir. Is that all?"

Troy prayed for strength, inhaled, and tried one more time. "Seaman Bonneville. Bonny. I've been in the infirmary all night, because I had to tell Lieutenant-Commander Lightner about PO Proctor. And it did not go well."

Bonneville kept his gaze on the floor. "Sorry, sir."

"The only break I took was to go call Proctor's family, because even though they'd heard from the hospital, they needed to hear from us. You can probably imagine how that went. And I still have to put together a memorial service before I leave for good. But if you would like to talk about what you – about what happened that night," he corrected himself, "my door is always open. I would really, truly like to hear about it."

After a miserable nod, the young man gathered his gear and paused at the doorway. "She couldn't have been there," he whispered. "It *couldn't* have been her. Dead is dead, sir." His anxious eyes fell on Troy's collar tabs. "Right? Dust to dust."

Troy's aching mind sought the right words, and the moment stretched on. At last he sighed. "Dismissed, Seaman."

"Sir." Bonneville nodded. "Tell the lieutenant-commander I'm sorry." Then he fled.

Troy hardly noticed as crewmembers in the passageway took one look at his expression and stood back to let him by. The reverberations of the deckplates beneath his boots seemed to shake his frustration loose to sift through his insides.

He waited four more days, but Bonny never came to see him. And by day two, Lightner stopped talking about what he'd seen.

☙

Civilian life – day three

"Have you decided where we're going yet?" Troy called, straightening his tie again.

"Ha. I decided weeks ago. I'm just not telling you."

He grinned, breathing in the scents of Maddy's shampoo and perfume on the moist air from the bathroom. There wasn't a trace of heavy steel or machine grease to be found, and he was still relishing the new reality.

"You all right?" Her voice was nearer now.

"Very much so." He opened his eyes and met her in the bathroom doorway, cupping her face in his hands. He was enjoying this, too – the sheer luxury of being close enough to touch. "And you are beautiful." He kissed her forehead.

"It's possible you're biased," she said. "But I guess I can live with that." She stood on tiptoe to kiss him properly, but after only a few pleasant moments, she pulled away with a sigh. "I should get ready."

"Why? That towel really brings out your eyes."

"Har har." She smiled at him anyway. "I just need ten minutes. Go keep Nate company until the babysitter gets here." His expression must've shifted, because she caught his hand. "Hey. Give him time, and give yourself some, too. The video calls were great, but you know they aren't the same as real life."

"I know. I know." He took a breath. "Okay, here I go. You take your time."

"Says the man who's already dressed and ready to go."

He followed the noise of falling blocks and roaring jet engines – or as roaring as a seven-year-old mouth could make them – to the den. He waited in the doorway, letting Nate get used to his presence, before saying, "Good grief, something terrible is happening to the city! Is that a Tyrannosaur?"

The boy shrugged, putting a dangerous wobble in the jet's flight path. "It's okay. The Air Force is coming to save them."

"Are you sure that's not a Navy jet?"

"Nope. Air Force," Nate said amiably.

"Well. They do good work. Can I help get the next one ready for takeoff?"

Nate hesitated only an instant before pointing at something that looked more like a spaceship than a jet. "Okay."

Smiling, Troy joined the fray. The city was almost safe again when the doorbell rang.

The girl on the front step stared up at Troy, clutching her pink knapsack close. He took a step backward, trying not to loom. "Hi," he said. "I'm Nate's dad."

"Hi," she managed. "Um. I'm Dylan."

"Come on in. Maddy's getting ready, so I think I'm supposed to show you where everything is."

"Um. I've been here before," she said as she trailed through the hall after him. "I kind of already know where everything is. Hey, Nate," she added as they passed the den.

"Hi, Dylan. The city got destroyed again! And guess what? Mom says we can order pizza!"

"Awesome!" She sounded so childishly pleased that Troy turned to consider her as they reached the kitchen. Under his scrutiny, she added, "The pizza, I mean. Not the city being destroyed. Obviously."

Suddenly, leaving his son with a stranger seemed like a terrible idea. Troy added the girl's long braided pigtails and that pink knapsack to his situation assessment. "How old are you, Dylan?"

"Seventeen. And I've done the babysitting course and everything," she added.

Do you have the diploma with you? he almost asked. *And some sort of photo ID?* "And you say you've been here before?"

"Um. Yeah." She noticed his expression. "Yes, sir. Lots of times."

"Any problems when you were here before?"

"At ease, sailor, you're scaring the poor girl. Hi, Dylan." Maddy shook her head at him as she stepped into the kitchen and laid a piece of paper on the counter, adding a twenty-dollar bill. "Okay: here's the money for the pizza. And I've added Troy's phone number to the list. You can use that or mine, which I know you already have." She cast a pointed look over the girl's head at Troy. "And on the very slim chance that neither of those work, the number of the restaurant's on here, too – we'll be at Villano's downtown."

"Aha. Good choice." Troy tried to sound friendly and harmless. "Here I was thinking you would've gone for Constantine's, but I like this even better."

Maddy and Dylan exchanged a glance. Then Dylan started studying the paper as if committing it to memory, and Maddy put a hand on Troy's arm.

"I thought I'd told you, hon. Constantine's burned down a couple months back. I'm so sorry – it must've slipped my mind somehow."

"Burned down?" For a moment his mental map of their neighbourhood tilted, and he was flailing. "Was – was anyone hurt?"

"No, it was four in the morning, some kind of electrical fault. No one was there. Everyone's safe."

"Safe. Good." He blinked memories of the infirmary away. "Good. But still a shame. I know you liked that place."

"They're already rebuilding." She smiled at him anxiously. "I can tell you the whole story over dinner. We'll add it to the list of things to catch up on."

"Yeah. Good. Sounds good."

"I'm going to go say good night to Nate," Maddy said, and Troy nodded. She squeezed his arm again.

Another silence fell as she left.

"So I brought *Scooby-Doo* to maybe watch tonight," Dylan said, pulling a slim case out of her knapsack. "The original cartoon, not that movie they did with real actors. I hope that's okay."

Troy pulled together a smile. "Probably. But you should ask Maddy. I don't even know if Nate likes *Scooby-Doo*." He tried a laugh.

"Well," Dylan said. "You've been gone for a while." She hastened on when he didn't respond. "It's just, we talked about it last time and she said Nate had never seen it, and I was like *whaaaat?* because it's such a classic. So I thought maybe now would be a good time."

He moved to the counter, aware that the girl's face was as anxious as Maddy's had been, and picked up the case. He still felt strangely off-balance, and the cartoon faces were rubbery and leering. He stared at them until they resolved into familiarity. "I used to watch this. You don't think it'll be too scary? You probably know him better than I do right now."

"Nah, he's a brave kid." She offered a hesitant smile. "Besides, the bad guys always turn out to be people just pretending to be ghosts and monsters and stuff. And even if the ghosts do turn out to be real, they're not that scary. They're cool."

"Ghosts are cool?"

"Sure. You get to come back and see your friends and family again, and they get to see you. That's pretty great."

He considered this. "Maybe."

"Troy," Maddy called from the hallway, "are you ready?"

"Yeah – just a sec." He held the case out to Dylan, but when she took it, he didn't let go. He straightened to his full height and gave her his best frown. "You're going to look after our boy for us, right, Dylan?"

"Yes, sir."

"Ghosts and all?"

"Yes, sir."

"Okay, then." Then he went into the other room, where the Army was helping to rebuild the city, and hugged his son good-night.

On the front stoop, he took a deep breath of air that had no trace of fuel tanks or salt water, just mown grass and a nearby barbeque. The houses were so close he couldn't see the horizon.

He handed the car keys to Maddy. "Could you drive? I think I'm… still finding my feet here."

She closed her fingers around his and squeezed. "You're doing fine."

They got in the car, but hadn't driven three blocks before he looked away from the landscape crowding his windows and focused on his wife's profile, shifting through light and shadow as the streetlights passed. "Do you believe in ghosts?"

She laughed once in surprise. "Ghosts? What kind of a question is that?"

"One I've never asked before," he said.

Civilian life – day thirty

Troy moved away from the library doors and stood for a moment, getting his bearings. He'd only ever been to their local branch library before, and this five-story monolith was almost overwhelming. He spotted a sign for the information desk and headed that way, trying not to feel guilty as he did so.

There was nothing to feel guilty about. He'd switched a shift at the youth centre to come here, that's all. He'd tell Maddy about it tonight at dinner, and by then he'd hopefully have something more interesting to report, too.

The information clerk directed him two stories up, to the non-fiction collection. He took the steps two at a time and realized he'd been letting his daily workout slide.

It's not as if Maddy would be angry about his coming here. Surprised, maybe. But he hadn't known the books would arrive so quickly. And it's not as if he had lied: he wouldn't do that. She was tolerating this new hobby of his pretty well. He could always call her.

No, it would be better to wait until dinner.

"Hi," he said to the woman at the non-fiction desk. "I ordered some books through library transfer and was told they were here to pick up. I have an order number if that helps." He handed it over, glad the slip didn't list the titles he'd ordered.

The librarian disappeared into the back office.

Surely people had ordered worse things through the library. Librarians wouldn't judge. She probably wouldn't even comment. It was a library, after all: people were supposed to be quiet. She'd just hand them over and he'd go work quietly at one of the tables in the far corner. No big deal.

"Ghosts, huh?" The voice seemed to echo for miles. "Nice."

Troy stared in horror at the young man putting a stack of books on the counter.

"Oh," the new arrival said, waving a hand at the back room. "I was the one who put this all together for you, so when Vi showed up with the slip I thought I'd bring them out, see who ordered them."

Troy looked around, saw – incredibly – no one watching them, and reached for the books, keeping his voice low in hopes this guy would do the same. "Thank you. For the books."

"No problem. You've got some good ones there – nice range of sources. The ones with the blue markers have to stay here. You can't take those home."

"Right, got it. Thanks." Troy started to turn away, eyes already on the furthest table.

"Whoa, hold on – you have to sign for them." The young man started searching through the desk papers, in no particular hurry. "Mind if I ask what you're working on?"

"Just a project."

The kid shrugged, sliding a piece of paper and a pen over the counter to Troy. "It's just that if you were only looking for regional ghost stories, or local legend stuff, I'd take a few of these out of contention. If you want the history of spiritualism and paranormal research, these two on top are your best options. But if you're actually doing investigations yourself, none of these will get you very far."

Troy blinked at him. "It's just… a general project. I'm sure these will be fine."

"Okay. Well, good luck with it." He started to turn away, but Troy thought he saw a trace of disappointment on his face, and for no good reason thought of Bonneville.

"Actually – " Troy took a deep breath, then sighed. "To be honest, I have no idea what I'm looking for. I've only recently started reading about this stuff." He couldn't help checking his perimeter again. No one was even looking in their direction. "I haven't ever really talked about it."

"Really? That's weird. But I guess it's whatever you're used to, right?" the young man said thoughtfully. "I had a friend in school whose parents would get really upset if he mentioned anything about ghosts or hauntings. Freaked out when he used a Ouija board at a party once, even though nothing happened. It was like they had this… certainty in their heads, about how life worked and how it ended, and they just wouldn't listen to any alternatives. Whereas my grandmother, for example, always swore she saw her brother die in Normandy during the war. She was in Boston at the time." He offered another shrug, adding a brief half-smile. "She taught chemistry at the college and went to Mass every Sunday. But something let her accept what she saw, and believe it."

"A crisis apparition." It was the kid's turn to look confused; Troy hadn't meant to say anything at all. "That's what it's called, when someone far away sees a friend or loved one appear around the time of death." He'd been eager to tell Lightner about it when he'd discovered the term, but Alex had ended the call as soon as Troy got the words out.

"Ah. I'd say death qualifies as a crisis, so that makes sense."

No, Troy thought, it doesn't make any kind of sense. Yet it seems to happen anyway.

"But if you already know that much," the young man was saying, "you might find a few of these books too simplistic. This is a lot to get through if you're not sure what you're looking for."

"I have time." Hesitating, Troy looked at the stack on the counter. "You said something about local legends? If I started there, which ones would help?"

Ten minutes later, he had a re-sorted pile, minus three books that probably wouldn't help at all, plus instructions for ordering microfiche back issues of local newspapers.

"And then there's the haunted walk," the young man said. "I think it starts at the old courthouse. I haven't done it, but I hear it's decent."

Troy laughed a little, picturing Maddy's reaction to that suggestion. "I think this stack of books and the microfiche will keep me busy for a while. But thanks. This whole conversation has been... very informative."

"Hey, it's the most excitement I'll have all day. So thank *you*. And if you need anything else, let me know. I work Monday to Friday, either here or in the back room. Just ask for Paolo."

"I'll do that," Troy said, and headed for the table in the middle of the room, where the light was best.

And if nosy library patrons looked over his shoulder?

Maybe they'd learn something.

Behind the Scenes

Now

Paolo tucked the laptop under his arm and let himself into his hotel room. He left his card key balanced on the door handle and crossed the room by the lights of the city below.

Turning on the lamp by the window, he wired his phone into the computer to start the picture-transfer process. Then he closed the curtains, poured himself a glass of water, and sat down with a sense of dread before the laptop's neat rows of new images.

The first twenty or so pictures from the convention were ones any fan might have, chaotically full of t-shirts, toys, buttons, posters and less identifiable wares crammed between people of all sizes, shapes, colours and costumes. He flipped through them until he got to the shots of the *OpHaunt* team waiting backstage before their session. Familiar faces mugged at him, pointing excitedly at their VIP passes or grimacing in exaggerated terror. Finally, he found what he was looking for – a series of three pictures taken fractions of a second apart.

He leaned closer and enlarged the final image.

Troy was blurry but identifiable on the left, while Dylan's head and shoulders were in perfect focus, filling the right side. She was turned in three-quarter profile, which was just enough to unleash the full force of the glare she was aiming at the camera… or more precisely, at him as the photographer. That glare called him *asshole* well before her voice could.

Other than that, it was a decent shot, given how quickly he'd had to act: her hair was gleaming under the stage lights, her face was glowing with excitement, and her mouth was as expressive as her eyes. Paolo took a moment to appreciate the composition before getting to work.

He opened the picture in a different imaging program, enlarged it to fullscreen and flipped through the editing menus until he found the filter he wanted. He realized he was muttering under his breath – "No, no, please no" – and clamped his jaw shut.

With a final click, the photo's colours downshifted into a moody palette that rendered Dylan's face almost unrecognizable. Now the light on her hair looked sickly against the violet smudge that curled around her head and shoulders like a monk's cowl.

Paolo sagged back in his chair. "Shit."

It was still following her.

(ᑎᑎ)

Five years ago

"Is Paolo around?"

When Troy's voice drifted through the open door, Paolo pushed away from his crowded desk. Thank God Troy was here – it meant this day was guaranteed to get more interesting. He left the stacks of books and headed out to the front counter.

"Good timing," Paolo said, shrugging on his coat. "Vi, I'm on lunch – be back in an hour." He stopped short a few paces later when he realized they weren't alone.

"Paolo, this is Rachel. You remember I told you about her? I've invited her to lunch with us. Rachel, Paolo."

She gave him a blinding smile. "Ah – so you're the reason Troy has duplicates of all his little ghost-finding gizmos. I've heard tales. Nice to finally meet you in person."

"Yeah. Likewise." After eight months of discovering similar interests, Paolo considered Troy a friend, but beyond a few stories, he had no reference for this girl. All the way down the stairs, he searched for something to say to her, feeling exposed and useless without his library counter and books. "So…uh. Rachel. You met Troy at the ghost walk?"

"Yeah. And I heard you suggested it." She grimaced. "Do me a favour and don't do that anymore, okay?"

"It wasn't that bad," Troy said. At her look, he sighed. "Okay, yes, it was."

"You never told me," Paolo said, feeling somehow both guilty and betrayed.

"It never really came up after I got distracted by Rachel's apartment thing. I told you about *that.*"

"Yeah, right. How's that going?" he asked Rachel.

"Great. Mr. Franklin is grumpy as ever and Murray the landlord's still confused, but Jeeves and I get along just fine."

"Jeeves?"

"It's what she named the ghost." Troy's voice was amused as they reached the front door. An elderly woman heading into the library looked up at him, startled. He smiled back at her as they stepped out into the wintry air.

"He tidies up after me and loiters near the door – I assume it's to announce visitors. What else would I call him?" Rachel pulled her mittens on and grinned at Paolo again, who couldn't think of anything clever to say back. He walked silently between them with his hands in his pockets, listening as she and Troy reminisced.

They were all settled in the cafe when Troy spoke again. "Okay. So the reason I wanted us all to meet is that I've had an idea, and I'd like you two to be in on it."

Paolo's wariness grew into disbelief as Troy proposed turning their mutual interest in local lore into an actual business. "Wait, what? You're… you want us to be ghostbusters?"

"Dibs on Venkman," Rachel said immediately. "He was hilarious. I can do that."

"I'm thinking less Hollywood, more helpful," Troy said to Paolo. "You and I both know how some people react to the supernatural: deny

117

and ignore. That doesn't help if they find themselves in a situation they can't explain, and it doesn't address the larger issue of the haunting."

"And we could? Even if we do find evidence of something, what are we supposed to do about it?"

"Well," Rachel said musingly. "First we'd have to build a containment unit in the basement —"

"No, seriously," Paolo interrupted, unease sharpening his tone. "Naming ghosts is fine if you want to live with them, but not everyone does. So we'd just tell those people, 'Yep, something's here, good luck with that'? It's not like we're exorcists."

Troy and Rachel exchanged a glance. "Actually —" Troy began.

Stung again, Paolo wished he were back at the library, back on familiar ground. "You're saying you *are*?"

"No," Troy smiled. "But Rachel has a background that gives her some insight into banishing and cleansing, and even though I'm not in an official role anymore, I am ordained by a recognized church. So if we had to, between our sources and your research skills, I imagine we'd be able to find a way to help."

"You must be joking."

"No. But I also imagine that mostly we'll find just regular people confronted by the unexplainable and wanting answers. Maybe between the three of us, we can give them some."

"I'm in," Rachel said. "The only job I've found so far is unbelievably boring. This sounds a lot more fun."

"Fun?" Paolo repeated. "Sure, finding all the old stories is great, and checking out abandoned sites can be interesting. But as a business, with strange people calling us up as clients? Do you know how many crank calls we'd get? And if they do turn out to be real, would they actually pay us to do this? How would we bill them? What if —"

"Hey, hey, slow down," Rachel said. "We can work out all those details as we go. But think of the amazing things we could see! This has potential. We start small here, help a bunch of people, and one day we'll be famous. World-famous ghost trackers."

"What? How? How could we *possibly* become famous for that?"

She waved a hand. "It'll happen."

Paolo stared at her confidence, and then at Troy's anticipation, and felt nothing but reluctance. "If you think I can help with the research, I can give it a shot. But – no offense – I'm not quitting my day job. And we'll need a better job description. I'm not listing my profession as 'ghost tracker' on a tax return."

"Wow." Rachel shook her head, but she was smiling. "You are just a walking ball of sunshine, aren't you?"

"No, that's you, Rache," Troy grinned. "We each have our own strengths. That's why this will work."

⑪

Now

The smell of stale beer and the noise of a hundred competing voices almost chased Paolo back out the bar door, but he gritted his teeth and pushed forward. Eventually he spotted the *OpHaunt* group seated in a corner banquette. They looked as if they were having a good time. Paolo hated to disturb them, but he needed Ben's help and knew he wouldn't be able to sleep until he had it. Plus, technically, he had been invited to join them. So he was probably going to have to sit a while and have a drink before he could even broach the subject.

Joy.

"Hey, there he is!" Rachel called out as he neared the table, drink in hand. "Where've you been? We expected you ages ago. Dylan's been here so long she's had a dozen shots and a case of beer."

"Slight exaggeration," Dylan said, tilting a half-empty pint glass in Paolo's direction. "Hi."

She seemed unsure how to act around him. He was used to that, after "the talk". Jasmine had been the same way after her version, though Ben had taken it more as a challenge than anything else. This time, though, Paolo felt as awkward as Dylan did. He couldn't help glancing at the top of her head, wondering if the entity was here now.

"Hi," he responded belatedly. Pulling his gaze away, he slid onto the end of the bench next to Ben, sending everyone scooting and shuffling. "What'd I miss?"

"The usual," Ben said. He was sitting close enough to Jasmine that their hands were probably touching under the table, but not so close as to trigger any rumours if a fan saw them. No one seemed to be paying attention, but unexpected photos from eagle-eyed bystanders showed up on the forums every week (*Spotted @ my grocery store!! guess he likes frzn pizza LOL*). Paolo let his face slide into the slightly bored detachment audiences expected of him, while the doctored photos on his phone burned a reminder through his pocket. He sat back, sipped his soda and braced himself for the wait.

It was painful. Troy hadn't joined them, and without his steady influence the group was a little too loud, a little too quick to laugh, reliving the best moments of the convention with sweeping gestures. Twice, fans ventured close for autographs, which always left behind a few moments' worth of weird, proud-embarrassed quiet. With the growing noise and crush of strangers filling the bar as the night wore on, Paolo's head was pounding. Finally he leaned toward Ben and shouted in his ear: "Ask your opinion about something?"

"What?"

Paolo held up his phone and nodded toward a somewhat quieter corner behind an unoccupied pool table. He elbowed his way through the crowd, and Ben joined him a moment later.

"Is this about work?" Ben asked. "Because we're supposed to be relaxing."

"Oh, admit it: you find work relaxing."

Ben shrugged and studied the picture on the phone Paolo handed him. "What's this?" He brought it closer, turning it toward the light.

Paolo wasn't sure what to say. He'd spent quite a bit of time cropping Dylan's face out of several pictures, so pretty much all Ben could see was the blob. If he now admitted he'd done that, wouldn't Ben wonder why?

He was still wondering himself.

"It's something I noticed a while ago, but it came up again while I was talking with Dylan tonight," he said carefully. "I thought it might be some sort of spirit shadow, but could it be just a flaw?"

"This is a filtered version," Ben said without accusation. "It's hard to say without seeing the original."

Paolo reached over and called up the next photo: the same cropped shot but without the colours edited. The cloudy form was completely absent, but the rest of the background was clearly the same.

"Ah." For a moment, Ben flicked back and forth between the two pictures, zooming in and out. "Hard to say for sure. Could be a shadow, like you said."

"What about this one?" With another reach and swipe, Paolo called up the next one.

"There are more?" The wrinkle between Ben's brows deepened as he compared the new filtered image to its unmodified original. "Well, it seems to be the same thing in each shot, anyway. Are these different rooms of a house?"

"Something like that."

Ben zoomed in again and peered more closely. "It's a strange shape, but someone's cut part of it off – the bottom and this arm disappear out of frame. And there's a strange lift in it, like it's molded up and over something. Who took these? Where are they from?"

"The archives." This time, Paolo saw, he'd given something away: Ben was frowning at him instead of the screen. "So you don't think this is a flaw in the camera? Some sort of... I don't know. Something?"

"It's too difficult to tell on here: the screen's too small and I don't have my software. And people are devious these days. You can email them to me and I can take a closer look on the plane tomorrow. Except you obviously want an answer now." He flicked back and forth between the pictures again. "All I can say is, it doesn't look like a lens problem. And flaws in film don't really happen now that everything's digital. Even if someone cut and pasted the same blob onto several pictures, they sure made an effort afterward to make some natural-looking changes." He handed back the phone. "So did I pass? Now can I know what's going on?"

"It wasn't a test." Paolo fidgeted under Ben's diagnostic stare. "Can I let you know when I figure it out myself?"

"Sure. But you should send them to me if you want a full analysis. Which I suspect you do, since it's the only reason you came out tonight."

"No, it isn't. We're celebrating our big day at the con."

Ben gave him a knowing look. "So you're coming back to the table?"

"Well." Paolo looked at the jostling crowd and then at his watch. "It's pretty late. And we have an early start tomorrow..."

"Hey, I'm only here because Jas wanted to come. But I'll tell the others where you went, if they ask."

They both knew the others wouldn't ask.

(ᵗᵇ)

Three and a half years ago

"Who's this guy?" Paolo whispered to Rachel as he joined her at what they called the conference table. We need a smaller table, he thought for the fiftieth time. And someone should water that plant.

"You know, you should really work on remembering people as well as haunting sites. That's Mitchell – he works for the production studio that did those TV specials with us. Lights, camera, action? Ring any bells?"

Paolo felt his face heat. Mitchell, at least, wasn't the one who had told Paolo about the viewers' response after the first special. That guy had been puffy and condescending under his sleek silver hair. This guy wasn't even Troy's age. He looked like an alert puppy, with a made-for-TV grin. Paolo's memory hesitantly placed him on the edges of meetings and in the shadows beyond the cameras.

Ben showed up and sat on Paolo's other side, trailing wires from the disembowelled gadget in his hand. He pulled a screwdriver from between his teeth when he saw Mitchell across the table. "Who's this guy?" he whispered.

But Troy had noticed Ben's arrival. "Oh, good. Let's get started."

Seeing the poorly-hidden excitement on Troy's face, Paolo had a sinking sense of déjà vu.

"Folks, it's really great to see you all again, and to finally meet you, Ben," the young man began. Paolo realized he'd never heard him speak before. "We've had some good times together already, and guess what? The ratings suggest that it wasn't just us, it wasn't just a fluke: people are watching, and they want to keep watching." He smiled sunnily, spreading his hands. "So we'd like to suggest a more permanent arrangement."

No, no, *no*, Paolo thought, as beside him Rachel crowed, "Yes! I knew it!" She pointed at Mitchell. "Are we going to be TV stars? We are, aren't we?"

He laughed, pointing back at her. "You jumped my gun. That's the plan, yes. We'd like *Operation: Haunting* to sign on for a partial season – thirteen episodes – with an option for more, depending on viewer response. How does that sound?"

Troy's and Rachel's responses were shining on their faces, so Mitchell turned his beaming face to the other two. Swallowing, Paolo tried to think of something to say.

"You want me to be on television?" Ben asked, sounding doubtful. "I've never done that before."

"You'll be great!" Mitchell said. "We really need your knowledge and skill. Our scriptwriters will make sure you can explain the technology in a way that viewers will understand."

"Scriptwriters?" Rachel repeated. "Wait – so this will be scripted? We'll be more like actors?"

Oh, *hell* no, Paolo thought, as his palms started to sweat.

But Mitchell was already shaking his head. "Your experiences in the field will be just what you're used to: set up, investigation, evidence review. All that won't change. Well, not much. But with a weekly show like this, we have to do some planning ahead, and we'll shoot additional footage for context. But that's a good thing, because it will give you a chance to tell the viewers about what you do and the tools you use. And of course we can show off the location, tell the history... All good stuff."

"Can we also show our results if we prove there's nothing super-natural happening?" Ben asked suspiciously. "We get more cases of sites that aren't haunted than ones that are."

"Of course we want those stories, too. They'll be educational. Though, cards on the table: I personally hope we get lots of real live hauntings!" Mitchell laughed again. "We'll have to be careful in our case selection, to be sure we get the goods. Sites with lots of documented history behind them." He nodded to Paolo. The others turned to him expectantly.

Paolo cleared his throat. "If you want me to do the research and maintain the archive, I will. But I'll do it behind the scenes. Not on camera." He could sense Troy's disappointment, but Mitchell was an unknown, his sunny, happy-puppy face too hard to read. Was that relief?

"Paolo –" Rachel began softly. He hated the sympathy in her voice.

"No, shut up," he said, sharper than he intended. Mitchell and Ben looked startled; Troy and Rachel exchanged a look Paolo recognized. "It's not a big deal. I'm better behind the scenes. Who needs to see the archivist anyway?"

"We need you on the ground, though," Troy said. "You're a good investigator."

"Not really," Paolo said. "Ben'll do better in my place. And I'll still come along to help set up and take down."

"But that leaves us with only three people actively investigating. That may not be enough."

"Ah, since you mention it," Mitchell put in, "we were going to suggest something. Your team is a little... skewed, demographically." He chuckled at their confusion. "We'd like you to hire another woman. For a weekly show like this, we'll need diversity. We'll lose audience share if we have too many men filling the shots. Not to be crass, but another pretty face can only help you here."

The team looked at each other, and Paolo saw uncertainty in Troy and Rachel for the first time. For a moment, he imagined them turning down the series and everything remaining exactly as it was now: their comfortable four-person team in their comfortable beige office, dealing with three little cases a week if they were lucky, reviewing evidence over take-out food, and occasionally – just occasionally – experiencing something incredible together.

Mitchell had noticed their hesitation, too. "Look at it this way: this would add to your appeal as well as giving you more investigators, if Mr. DeSanto really does want to stay behind the scenes. Ultimately, of course, it's up to you, but cards on the table: this hiring idea isn't just coming from me, some little guy on the ground. This is a recommendation from some pretty important and experienced folks at the studio. They think it's a smart idea, and they're willing to make sure you're in a financial position to do it so we can make this show happen."

And Paolo knew it was all over.

Feeling hollow, he listened to Mitchell enthusiastically explain the rest of the deal, watched the others sign their contracts, and finally scrawled his signature on his own copy, squeezing the pen to hide his shaking hand.

Rachel touched his shoulder lightly. "Try to see the good in this, sunshine. It'll mean amazing things. Promise."

He managed a nod, and she followed Ben out of the room.

When at last Paolo handed the papers to Mitchell, the man's toothy grin widened. "Fantastic. Glad to have you on board in any capacity, and I mean that. Now listen, I didn't intend to eavesdrop, but – 'sunshine'? Is that what the team calls you?"

"No." Only Rachel, Paolo thought, when she thinks I need it.

"Are you sure? Could it be?"

"No." He practically snarled it.

Mitchell blinked, and tried again. "It would really endear you to the audience…"

"I'm just the archivist. I don't need to be endearing," Paolo said, and escaped.

✿

Now

The early morning sun was gaining strength as Rachel knocked on his door. He pulled her into his room, talking over her half-hearted protests. "Finally. Didn't Troy tell you not to have a late night? We have to leave in half an hour."

"Which is why I was planning on twenty more minutes of sleep. What's the big emergency?"

"You need to see something."

She blinked blearily at him over her coffee cup while he opened the first image file on his laptop and explained at top speed. "I saw this on the thermal initially, at the Yorkside Jail. But look, this is two weeks later. I was adjusting the light levels to post this clip on the site. I chose the wrong filter and there it was." He opened another file. "And this one's taken with the still camera, from an episode during the contest. It's there with her, every time. Even yesterday." When Rachel didn't immediately respond, he showed her the picture from the convention.

Finally she sat forward, frowning at the screen. "What is that?"

"I don't know! I thought it was just a spirit at the jail! I didn't think it could follow her. Have you ever heard of that happening?"

"Okay, take a breath. How many of these do you have?"

"After I went back and checked them all? Twenty-one – well, twenty-two after yesterday. All different dates, different locations. Whatever it is, it isn't just a coincidence."

She slid her gaze sideways at him. "She's only been with us for a season. Did you take that many pictures of the other contestants?"

"Could you focus? She could be in real trouble here."

"From what? Apparently it's already been there for months."

"And God knows what it's doing to her! It could be... influencing her somehow without her knowing. Draining her energy, playing with her mind. It could – I don't know, push her down the stairs? Choke the life out of her, maybe?" Rachel's sudden glare was icy cold, and he backed off. "Look, even if it's not as bad as what happened to Jas, it can't be good. Spirits are energy, and this thing was drawn to her from the start. So what does it want? Why is it staying? Why *her*?"

"Ah," Rachel said softly. "There he is."

"What?"

"The man behind the Paolo. Crushing pretty hard, isn't he?"

"*What?* No. Shut up."

"Whatever, sunshine."

"Rachel: Dylan has some kind of entity following her around, and it first appeared in one of the darkest, most violent places we have ever been. Don't you think that's a little more important right now than a crush? Which I don't have," he added through gritted teeth, "because I'm not twelve."

Her gaze returned to the screen. "How sure are you about this... entity?"

"Really, really damn sure. I even had Ben check some of the images. Sort of."

"Okay, then. You're right – we should talk to her. Have you told Troy?"

"No. I wanted to be sure, and he seemed pretty exhausted last night."

"So I'll do that. You talk to Dylan." She stood, then noticed his expression. "Problem?"

"No," he hedged. "I already told her to be careful, but I don't know if she took me seriously. It's kind of an awkward topic to bring up again. Like, 'Say, remember that weird occult cloud from the jailhouse?'"

"Call it a safety issue, show her the photos. Just tell her you're concerned about her."

"That we're concerned. The whole team."

"Right." She paused at the door. "Word of advice – for this conversation, make sure you're OH_Boy instead of Paolo, okay?"

"They're the same person," he protested as she left.

"No, they aren't," her voice called from the hallway, and the door clicked shut.

He scowled, then sighed.

Here was the thing about Rachel: she knew stuff.

Paolo thought it was some sort of genetic confidence hardwired into her DNA. Ben thought she was just really observant. Jasmine swore it was ESP. Whatever caused it, Rachel knew things. Sometimes she'd say something, but it was only later, only if you'd been paying attention, that you'd realize she was right.

Except that one time, Paolo thought. She hadn't known about the Mortimer house, and now she'll never forgive herself.

He forced his mind back to the present and found himself again the target of Dylan's frozen glare. The sight of the hovering purple shadow made him queasy. He tried to plan the conversation they had to have, but now, with Dylan's picture in front of him, and his memories of how nervous she had been onstage, and then how she'd relaxed enough to laugh and joke, and then how surprisingly cool her skin had been when he'd reached past his fear to warn her last night, he eventually had to admit something else.

Rachel was probably right about that, too.

(♏)

Two and a half years ago

"So it's true? We're actually going to Europe? For real? Ooh, ooh - are we doing the Paris catacombs? Or the Tower of London?" Jasmine's eyes were wide with excitement as she snatched a copy of the itinerary.

"Yes to the Tower, after superhuman negotiation. *Maybe* to the catacombs," Mitchell smiled proudly. His usual sunniness was practically blinding this morning.

"I'm going in solo. I'll try out the helmet cam," Jasmine said immediately, and didn't wait for his answer. "Holy cats, we're going to Europe! This is going to be so amazing. I *love* this job!"

Paolo winced at the upward squeal of her voice, but looking around the table, he decided she'd only expressed what the others were thinking. She tended to do that. Everyone was grinning like fools. For the first time in a long time, he'd been listening to Mitchell with excitement rather than dread.

"Okay, assignments," Troy said. "Rache, let's wrap up last week's stuff and get those invoices done before we go. Paolo, don't say anything online yet, but keep gathering pictures and information, and send us anything we should know before we leave. Jasmine, could you help Ben square away the equipment and make a full inventory for customs?"

"Sure thing," she said. "Maybe if I actually help pack it all, I'll be able to find what I need when I need it."

"You should always be able to find what you need," Ben protested as they both stood to leave. "That's why we bought those custom suitcases."

"Well, I don't know how you organize them, but it's always a scavenger hunt. Do you pack them alphabetically, or by amperage, or what?" She jostled his arm teasingly.

Rachel watched them leave before turning back to her laptop with a grin. "Think he's noticed yet?"

"Noticed what?" Mitchell asked.

"She's not exactly subtle about it," Troy said.

"He wouldn't notice unless she dressed up as a circuit board," Paolo said absently, scrolling through images of the Paris catacombs on his own screen. "A sexy circuit board," he added.

"It worries me that you've already thought of that." Rachel shook her head. "Mitchell, quick question: could we add one more case here before we head out?"

He made the face he always made when the answer was no. "I don't think that's in the budget or the timeline, Rachel. Sorry."

"What's up?" Troy came to look over her shoulder.

"Email from a family with two kids out on the east coast. Sounds active." Rachel's frown was half a wince. Paolo wondered how bad her WiFi headache was.

"A family case?" Mitchell made another of his faces. "Cards on the table, guys, they aren't usually our most watchable episodes."

"We started out investigating private homes," Troy said evenly. "They're mostly why we got into this business in the first place. Looks like this" – he checked the screen again – "Mortimer family is having some trouble."

"Troy, I get it, I really do, and it's great you want to help ordinary folks. But there's no time before you go to Europe, and the season's booked pretty solid after that."

Troy and Rachel studied the screen and murmured for a while, but Paolo wasn't surprised when Troy finally sighed. "Flag it. I'll write back with apologies, and tell them we'll do our best to get there before the end of the season." He looked at Mitchell, who was opening his mouth to protest. "And we will do our best."

"Send me their address," Paolo suggested. "Maybe we know a local team to recommend in the meantime."

"Sunshine, you soft-hearted genius."

Troy nodded at Paolo, then picked up a copy of the itinerary. "Give me a few minutes, Rache – I want to call Maddy about Europe." He left, and the only noise in the conference room was the rapid clicking of computer keys.

Paolo gradually became aware that Mitchell was watching him. "Now what?"

"You know, sometimes it's almost like you're two different people," Mitchell said musingly. "Anytime we put you onscreen, you're prickly. Cactus man. Hard to talk to, hard to like."

"Thanks," Paolo said.

"But one-on-one, here with the group, you're fine. I don't get it. Look, I'm not trying to be offensive here…"

"You're not even trying? Wow."

Mitchell squinted at him. "I only mention it because there is one more thing I wanted to talk to you about today. In private," he added.

Paolo exchanged a glance with Rachel. Nodding, she settled back in her chair, looking at Mitchell expectantly.

The studio man hesitated again. "Paolo, we'd like you to be on camera more often. Starting with the Europe trip." Mitchell held up a hand. "Hear me out: you give the histories of the sites and all the reports of activity in the best possible way, and you don't even need a script for it. So you're valuable there. But we're also starting to see some audience feedback that indicates they don't mind the... prickliness." Seeing Paolo's disbelief, he shrugged. "Seriously. Some people seem to think it gives you character. Focus groups are telling us it's a nice contrast against, say, Troy. And especially against Rachel."

Rachel snorted dismissively.

"We think it'll work," Mitchell went on. "And Europe would be a great place to get you back into investigating. Like a clean slate."

"A clean slate for me to be cranky on?"

"Well, the thing is, people are used to you now. They expect it, and apparently a bit of crankiness is like a breath of fresh air. Haven't you seen the fan forums?"

Paolo, who tried his best to avoid them as much as possible, shifted in his seat. "Not every single post."

"Well, you should see what they say. They want more of you, cactusman. In fact, I think you could play it up a little and they'd still go for it. You're more comfortable with the cameras, and how the show works, and you've got a good team going here. So now's the time. Think about it, okay?" He nodded to them and left the room.

In the new silence, Paolo was startled to discover that the thought of being on camera more often didn't make him break out in his usual cold sweat. But the rest of the suggestion had made his insides twist, and he couldn't quite figure out why.

"You can't do this," Rachel said, shaking her head.

"The focus groups seem to think I can."

"Bullshit. Don't let them push you into this – into being what you're not." He raised his eyebrows at her, which she ignored. Her voice stayed low and vehement. "Jas is working out great, so we have enough investigators. We do not need anything else to fill a damn hour of television. You do plenty for this team, more than enough, behind the cameras. You're already obsessing with the archives and the site and everything else –"

"You're exaggerating. I'm not obsess–"

131

"No? How much sleep did you get last night?" she asked, and nodded when he scowled in response. Her voice softened a little. "Don't do this. It's so unfair."

"It's not like it's going to take over my life! If it'd be good for the show – for the team – maybe I should do it." When she started to protest, he waved her silent. "Look, Rache, I admit: when this all started, I thought it was a bad idea. I really don't like change, and I really don't like new people." He risked a glance at her and saw no surprise, only acceptance. "But I had learned to fake it at the library, and here in the office, and with Ben and then Jas, and then somehow I got used to it, and now I genuinely like where we are. So if I can help keep that going, why wouldn't I?"

"You're already keeping us going. A new version of Paolo isn't necessary."

"Rachel," he said as he closed his laptop, "We chase ghosts for a living. None of what we do is *necessary*. This is just a part of it. So maybe I play up the snark a little – it's not like that's hard for me. Besides, fake it 'til you make it, right? Isn't that the first commandment of reality television?" Paolo tried a smile, but she didn't respond. He reached out and patted her shoulder awkwardly. "Don't worry. I'll get used to it."

She just shook her head, uncharacteristically silent, so he left to find Mitchell.

⑪

Now

Paolo took a deep breath and gestured at the aisle seat. "Mind if I join you?"

Dylan turned away from the window, startled. "Uh, that's actually Rachel's seat. I think she's just in the bathroom."

"Yeah, but then she showed up wanting to talk to Troy, so she's in my seat for a while." He flattened himself backward to let the attendant pass with the drinks cart. "So would it be okay if I sat here?"

"Um, sure. Go ahead."

"Great." He folded himself into the aisle seat, still wondering how he was going to do this. There weren't a lot of people nearby to notice if things went horribly wrong, but the white noise of the engines meant he had to lean half-over the empty seat between them to be heard. Awkward on so many levels, Paolo thought, and cast about for an opening. "So. How are you feeling this morning?"

Dylan looked confused. "Fine."

"I just meant – because of the bar. I mean, of course Rachel was just kidding about the drinking. But you know, big day, couple of drinks, late night, early morning…" He tried to stem the babbling, but he was already distracted by the thought of that entity, lurking in some invisible spectrum but still there. Could spirits travel by plane? Would the pressure change affect them?

"Right," Dylan said when he finally trailed off. "Well, it turns out I can handle a pint and a midnight bedtime just fine, actually." She sounded torn between amusement and irritation. Noticing his attention, she lifted a hand to her head. "Do I have something in my hair?"

"What? No, nothing. Just… I thought I saw something outside."

She sent a doubtful glance out the sky-filled window, then back at him. "Are *you* okay?"

"Yeah, sure. Fine." His nerves jangled through the moment of silence.

"Were you up late yourself?" Dylan asked. "I know you didn't stay long at the bar. But was there a lot to do after the con? Putting up pictures and posting on the forums or whatever? Doing all that plus the archives and records must take a lot of time." She said it as if she'd never thought of it before, eyeing him. "And you post a lot on the forums. The others say you don't seem to sleep at night."

He grimaced. "They worry too much."

"Maybe. Or they just care about you." Then she added, with a curl to her mouth that matched her faintly teasing tone, "Can't imagine why."

"I know, it's weird. Mass delusion? My natural charm? It's a mystery." This earned him an actual laugh, and he relaxed a fraction. "We do tend to look out for each other, though."

"Yeah. It's nice."

In the next instant, all Paolo's half-formed strategies evaporated, and his words just spilled out. "About what happened in the Yorkside Jail – I wish I could've told you what I saw in the thermal. I almost did, a hundred times, while it was happening."

Dylan stiffened in her seat, but he couldn't stop now that he'd started.

"And I could blame it on someone else, because the powers-that-be suggested ages ago that we not make too big a fuss over seeing anything at the time we see it. They probably told you the same during the contest: downplay your reactions, in case the footage doesn't make the final edit. But after Jasmine's accident, we decided as a team we had to do something, so between ourselves we came up with little code phrases to let each other know if something was going on, but not give it away to the audience."

She was already staring, but now her eyes widened further. "You –"

"As soon as I said something was off, the way I said it, Troy knew," Paolo said. "He knew I could see something. But I couldn't tell him specifics. Then, when you started... reacting, and I said 'not a damned thing', he knew it was still there and he had to get you out, fast." He finally paused for breath, and she looked so betrayed he wanted to disappear. "I am so sorry."

She was sitting statue-still, only the ends of her hair moving under the air vents. Then she seemed to pull herself together. "Okay. I guess."

"There's more," Paolo managed to say. Pulling out his phone, he called up a filtered but uncropped photo, with her shadowy face just visible below the violet smudge. "This was two weeks later."

Paolo watched Dylan's expression fall, but forced himself to swipe the screen for the next image, and the next, and the next, until she turned away. "When we were filming in the jail, I thought it was responding to you, but it's more than that," Paolo said. "It's following you. It was there yesterday at the con – it might be here right now." She darted a glance at him, too quick to decipher. "It could be dangerous. We have to find a way to get rid of it."

She stilled again. "No." At his look of confusion, she added, "I'm sure it's nothing. I'm fine."

"No? But Dylan –" He started fumbling with his phone, searching for yesterday's picture and ignoring the sudden chill down his spine.

"Paolo," she said, sharply enough to stop him. "I'm fine. There must be some other explanation."

"What else can it be? Look, we'll get the team on it, I'll email these to Ben –"

"I said no."

He could only gape at her.

Her voice lost some of its edge. "But I appreciate your concern."

"This – this thing could be doing anything to you! You might not even realize –"

"I am fine," she said with slow emphasis. "And you don't know me well enough to tell me I'm wrong about that. So you're going to have to believe me."

Paolo sought some new argument in the face of her certainty, but eventually, all he could do was slide out of the seat. "Fine. But I'm not going to watch you end up like Jasmine. So if you need help, you speak up, okay? Tell Rachel, or Troy, or... someone." He turned his phone over and over in his hands, so frustrated he couldn't meet her eyes. "And I'm still sorry. I would do anything to change that day in the jail."

As he left he thought he heard Dylan mutter, "Shit."

But it was probably just the noise of the engines.

The team was groggy and out of sorts after a day of travel and a mediocre dinner, but they all stirred to life as Troy turned off the main road and the van started down a narrow tree-lined laneway, through tiger stripes of sunset and shadow. He pulled up in front of a tall, sprawling grey house, vine-strewn and sagging at the edges, dark except where the dying sun touched its upper windows.

135

Troy shut off the engine and got out without saying a word. The rest of the team piled out into the driveway, looking up at the house as the forest rustled behind them.

"Jinkies," Rachel said.

What is this place? Jasmine signed.

"Shequand Manor," Paolo said. "Originally built in the 1830s. The Shequands owned it for generations. The flu epidemic in 1919 wiped out nearly all their neighbours, businesses and most of the family. Maude Shequand and her son Titus survived, but pretty much kept to themselves until the mid-sixties. Titus died first and Maude soon after, but it was a while before anyone found them. Then the estate went to some cousins who really didn't have the money to upkeep it properly, and the next generation didn't want to stay. They rented it out for a while but it's been essentially empty for at least a decade." He studied the peeling shutters and crumbling brick. "Local kids say –"

"Belay that," Troy interrupted, smiling faintly. "Let's not spoil it for everyone."

The team looked from him to Paolo and back again. "You two set this up?" Rachel asked, sounding pleased and surprised.

"Not me," Paolo said. "I found it and sent a proposal to the studio, but they turned it down."

"Screw the studio," Troy said, holding up an old key. "This one's just for us. We deserve it." He opened the back of the van and tossed an old duffel bag to the ground. "Here's the tech."

"That's it?" Ben was aghast.

Jasmine laughed silently at him, hugging his arm in excitement.

"Take whatever gadgets you want, or none at all," Troy said, unzipping the duffel. "Though I do think we should each have a two-way radio and a flashlight as well as our phones. We have no idea what the interior conditions will be like. We'll have to be careful where we step." He smiled over at Paolo and Rachel. "Just like old times."

"Only the walkie and a flashlight for me, then," Rachel said with a delighted laugh.

By the time they'd sorted themselves out, darkness had pooled on the front porch and fireflies were blinking in the yard, but the excitement had caught everyone. Paolo felt like they were skipping school to do something they shouldn't.

"Wait, wait," Ben said suddenly. "Don't we need assignments? Do we team up?"

Let's just go! Jasmine signed.

"No, Ben's right – otherwise we'll be tripping over each other." Troy thought a moment, then looked at Ben and Jasmine. "You two take the ground floor to start. Rachel and Dylan can take the second floor, and Paolo and I will check out the third. Agreed?" Nods all around. "Check in an hour from now if not before, and maybe we'll rotate." Nods again. "So what the heck are you waiting for? Go, go –" He laughed as Jasmine snatched the key out of his hand and bolted for the door, Rachel and Dylan not far behind and Ben startled into chasing after them.

Troy and Paolo stood for a moment longer, watching the flashlight beams dance suddenly in the windows and listening to the excited voices recede as the team reacted to the house.

"Headed upstairs," Rachel's voice said in a loud, unsettling stereo as both their two-way radios flared on. Troy winced and turned his down. "Watch your step, they're mushy. And just so everyone knows: headache's setting in." She sounded pleased.

The radio channel chirped again. "Safety note: rotten floorboard to the inside right of the dining room door," Ben's slightly breathless voice said. "And I've already got a two-point-seven on the EMF, Rache."

Troy and Paolo's phones chimed simultaneously, alien in the quiet yard. Troy pulled his out, tilting it so Paolo could read Jasmine's mass text. *Wallppr = face-like paisley dsign. Any reprts of visions in liv rm so totally #debunked*

"Well," Troy said as he and Paolo picked their way across the darkened porch and stepped into the house. "Maybe not exactly like old times."

☊

Seven months ago

"You're sure it won't seem like it's been rigged?" Troy sounded worried, but Mitchell was shaking his head.

Paolo was only half-listening. Most of his mind was filled with an anxious roar of white noise as he risked another peek at the crowd. The team was huddled on a riser at the front of the room, and beyond them the season's twenty contestants and their plus-ones were milling around in excitement, chattering in groups and stealing glances at the team. Paolo stepped closer to Ben and Jasmine, who were signing intently to each other with their backs to the audience.

"What's the issue?" Rachel asked Troy.

"My son's old babysitter. She made the top twenty. I didn't even know she entered, I swear – we haven't seen her since she left for college." He offered a little wave toward the audience. A handful of eager contestants waved back. "That's her near the window, in the blue shirt."

"It's fine," Mitchell soothed.

"It's serendipity," Rachel smiled.

"It's a disaster waiting to happen," Paolo said, more loudly than he'd intended. He glared at Mitchell and lowered his voice. "This whole contest has reeked of a ratings-grab since day one. Do you know how close I am to actually getting us access to the Yorkside Jail before it's gone forever? Do you know how huge that is? And now you want me to tell them that we might be bringing some teenybopper amateur along like it's a school field trip?"

"All contestants had to be over twenty-one," Mitchell began. "They've each signed a waiver –"

"Dylan would be, what, twenty-two by now? Twenty-three?" Troy murmured, still worried and distracted.

"You're not much older than that, sunshine," Rachel pointed out. "They're not children."

"Missing the point," Paolo growled. He looked out over the audience again and saw their conversation had drawn attention. Some of the contestants were muttering, others falling silent. The young woman in blue was standing a little apart, watching the stage with a faint smile. Her eyes met Paolo's with open curiosity.

"It's a terrible idea," he said, turning away from her and all the other strangers. "But I've done what you wanted and taken the damn pictures for the website, so I'm out of here. Do this part without me." He pushed through their burst of whispered protests.

Careful not to run, he left the stage under the unnerving weight of what felt like a thousand eyes. Somehow, the babysitter's lingered longest.

⟨th⟩

Now

A third of Shequand Manor's topmost floor had been converted into smaller rooms – servants' quarters, Paolo thought, once they found the steep back staircase and tiny bathroom. The servants were long gone but the bedroom walls were scrawled with recent graffiti, the floors drifted with scraps of clothing, crumpled beer cans and dried cigarette butts. The rest of the storey, once Troy forced the door open, was a long echoing storage space the full width of the house. Someone had written WELLCOME on a spotted mirror propped half-facing the door, but a few paces onward, the dust carpeting the floor seemed undisturbed. The thick cobwebs looked years old. In the brassy light struggling through the windows, it was a maze of household debris hiding under dropcloths or stacked haphazardly between animal droppings.

Troy and Paolo split up to explore, the floorboards creaking and moaning as they went. "This might explain what some people say they hear on the second floor," Paolo said, easing his foot up and down to produce a loud, human-like complaint.

"Except it doesn't look like anyone's been up here for a while." As Troy neared the middle window, a burst of frenzied movement sent him ducking aside. The frantic little black blot squeaked faintly as it disappeared into a gap beneath the eaves. "I don't miss the bats," he muttered.

On the other side of the room, Paolo was looking around with a frown. "Do you smell that?"

"I smell bat," Troy said. "And dust. And whatever else has been using this room as a nest-slash-toilet."

"No, this is –" Paolo took another breath, trying to get past everything Troy had just named, "flowers?"

Troy started to wind his way toward him. In a far corner, something scrambled away on tiny pattering paws. Paolo pulled a grimy sheet off the nearest pile, and for a few moments the resulting cloud of dust kept both of them coughing and blind. When it settled, they were blinking at a low chest of drawers and a mattress-less crib on tall spindly legs, crowned with equally spindly rails.

"This would not pass a safety inspection." Troy tested a rail and a piece broke off between his fingers. "Called it."

"There it is again," Paolo said. He leaned over the crib, sniffing carefully. "Can't you smell it? Flowers. I can't tell what kind."

"As a parent, I can assure you babies do not smell like flowers." Troy brought the broken piece to his nose. "It's not the wood."

"Is it something in the drawers?" As carefully as he could, Paolo worked the top drawer of the chest open. It was empty.

"Maybe a window's open." Troy moved toward the nearest one. "Holy –" He shied backwards, knocking over a broken easel and sending up more dust with the clatter.

"What?" Paolo coughed. "What happened?"

"Sorry – false alarm. Sorry. I caught a reflection in the window of that mirror by the door, and thought I saw something move."

"A reflection of a reflection? Rookie mistake."

"Yeah, don't tell anyone – I could never hold my head up again." He exhaled. "But that mirror's creepy, right?"

The room darkened further as they considered the mirror. This time, they both exclaimed when a shadowy form appeared across its surface.

Then a flashlight beam swept toward them, and the figure in the mirror doubled as Rachel joined Dylan in the doorway. "Guys?"

"How about a little warning next time?" Paolo snapped.

"We told you we were coming up," Rachel retorted, holding up her radio. "Not our fault you didn't answer."

Both men reached for their walkies, clicking through channels of utter silence. "Dead," Troy said.

"Batteries?"

"I charged them all before we went to dinner."

The four of them looked at each other for a moment, then Rachel nodded. "Looks like you were right, newbie. It was Dylan's idea to come up," she added, her tone as light as ever. It was hard to read her expression in the gloom, but Paolo knew she was looking significantly at him and Troy. "She had a feeling something was happening up here. The radio silence pretty much confirmed it."

"Good instincts," Troy said.

"Sorry we startled you. Though it was pretty funny," Dylan snickered, playing her flashlight beam around the attic with interest. Rachel, Paolo and Troy exchanged another glance, again more felt than seen, and Rachel rubbed the base of her skull.

"Guys," she said, "this headache's getting vicious. Ben's got the only EMF, but I proclaim this a hot spot. Not sure I can stay much longer."

"Let's switch it up," Troy suggested. "You and I can head back downstairs, and Dylan and Paolo can stay up here."

Dylan's surprise turned to dismay, quickly hidden. Paolo scowled. Rachel traded her radio for his dead one, insisting that hers had worked perfectly as of five minutes ago, and Troy told Dylan to be careful. Then they disappeared into the servants' hallway and clattered down the stairs as the last glimmers of sunlight faded from the air.

There was a long moment of silence in the new dark. Whatever it was rustled in the corner again. Dylan shifted uneasily, her flashlight beam jumping into jagged life.

"So," Paolo said, trying for natural. "Do you smell flowers here?" He clicked on his own flashlight, shining it on the crib in front of them.

"Flowers?" She moved carefully closer. Her flashlight flicked up toward his face as if checking for mockery. He heard her take a deep breath. "Hmm."

"And?"

"Yeah," she said slowly. "Like a perfume my gran used to wear. Old-fashioned. Lily of the valley, maybe?"

"Maude? Is that you?" Paolo called into the dark. "We aren't here to hurt anyone. But if you'd like to talk to us, we'll listen."

Whatever was huddled in the corner rustled as if in response. When he sent his flashlight beam toward it, crazy shadows chased themselves across the mirror by the door. He paused, swept back and found the mirror again, trying to light it without a glare.

"I think it's just an animal," Dylan whispered.

"In the corner, yeah. But that mirror…" Paolo raised his voice again. "Maude? Was that your mirror? Are we in your way?" He took a step, then whispered over his shoulder at Dylan. "Did you just feel a draft?"

"It's – I'm not sure this is Maude," she said.

"What makes you say that?" He finally found a way to light the surface of the mirror just enough to see the room reflected. He held the flashlight as still as he could.

"You said the family lived here for generations. Anyone could still be around." Dylan sounded distracted. "Tell me about the flu epidemic – do we know who died here?"

Paolo searched his memory while he kept his eyes on the mirror. "Uh… Maude's husband Bernard, and his uncle Richard, who had been staying with them. The three youngest children – eight-year-old twins and a toddler, no names given. Oh, and Maude's –"

A shadow darted across the mirror, though the room was still.

"Did you see that?" Paolo hissed. "It happened when I said her name. Maude, is that you?"

"I don't think so – I think this is tied to the epidemic," Dylan whispered. "Downstairs we heard someone coughing."

"So maybe she got sick like everyone else, but survived it. Maude? Can you tell us what happened?"

"But that doesn't make sense," Dylan murmured. "Why would she be up here?"

"It seems active around this crib. She did lose three children."

Paolo and Dylan stared at the crib while the scent of flowers drifted around them. They listened to the silence for a while, and when a faint cough sounded from the hallway, they both turned to look.

"What about the servants?" Dylan prompted. "Did any of them die of the flu?"

"Uh, maybe. I think there was a mention, but I was more focused on the family."

She shook her head at him. "Classist snob. I bet at least one servant died: the nanny. She would've been around the children every day."

Another cough reached them. A muted clatter suggested a pile of debris in one of the servants' rooms had gone sliding.

"I'm sorry – we don't know your name," Dylan said, just loudly enough to carry. "But we appreciate you being here to look after the children. I was a babysitter myself." She laid a careful hand on the crib railing. "I know how easy it is to get attached. And I'm sure you did your best when they got so sick."

Suddenly certain that something was rushing him from behind, Paolo whirled around. His flashlight showed only empty room, empty doorway, empty hallway. Once again, the back of his neck tingled with cold, but it was Dylan who shivered. And seeing that shake of her shoulders, a half-dozen memories since the Yorkside Jail rearranged themselves in Paolo's mind.

Dylan and Paolo each stood still and mute as the fragrance of flowers gathered again, nearly strong enough to taste. Slowly it faded into the silence around them.

Paolo's fingers found the phone in his pocket. In the pale backwash of the flashlights, Dylan still seemed distracted: her head was tilted and she was smiling a little, as if she were listening to good news.

At last she looked up, with a satisfaction that made his chest ache. "Well, she's not hurting anyone, whoever she is. I say we let her be. But nice job – I think we figured this one out."

Paolo didn't take his eyes from her as he tapped on the camera icon and took a picture. The flash blinded them both.

"Ow! Ow, *damn* it, Paolo! What the – "

"It's here right now, isn't it?" Paolo demanded, furiously blinking bright spots away. "It is, and you know it. You say 'we figured this one out', but you mean 'we' as in, you and it. Working together somehow. Is it… is it *talking* to you?"

There was a long, breathless pause.

"Don't look at me like that." Dylan's voice was so low he could hardly hear it. "This is exactly why I didn't want to say anything."

Paolo tried to stifle a shudder of his own as ice trailed cross his shoulders again.

"Now you're just freaking him out. Stop it," Dylan said, but not to him. "He might be a total jerk sometimes, but he's not stupid." She met Paolo's horrified eyes. "Please don't tell anyone."

He managed a strangled laugh. The animal in the corner snuffled at them.

"Don't, Paolo. It'll change everything. The rest of the team is still getting used to me. We just made the big announcement," she said plaintively. "I just signed the contract. Please? I want to stay."

"You think this is about a *job*?" His incredulity echoed through the attic, sending the animal scuttling. "The job is the least of your worries. This thing is dangerous!" What felt like a frozen fingertip jabbed his cheekbone. "Stop it," he snapped, waving away nothing he could see.

"It's not dangerous! It's keeping me safe!" Dylan seemed embarrassed once she'd said it. "It's not dangerous. I promise."

"Wow," Paolo said after a moment. "There's a whole story behind that. But this isn't like a stray dog, Dylan. It wraps itself around your *head*. We don't know what it might be doing to you."

"Don't treat me like a child," she snapped. "I'm telling you it's fine, and has been fine for months now. It makes me a better investigator."

"You were a good investigator all on your own!"

"I didn't say I wasn't. I said this makes me *better*." They were both silent for a while, scowling at each other. Then Dylan spoke again, more calmly. "I am asking you not to tell the others. Call it professional courtesy."

"Not my strong point, as you might've noticed. No way. They need to know."

Paolo's radio buzzed into life, Ben's voice startling them both. "Guys? Uh. Jas and I have pretty much covered the ground floor, and we caught a few things, but it's been a long day – I don't know if we have the energy to do a lot else. We might just wait in the van if you guys want to keep going."

Another click, and Rachel's amused voice responded. "You two are like an old married couple already. Hate to ruin your alone time in the van, but Troy and I were just thinking we could wrap this up. Attic team?"

After a moment, Dylan nodded stiffly and Paolo opened the channel. "We're done. See you in a few." He put the radio away and headed toward the door. He'd just felt the cooler air of the hallway on his face when Dylan spoke again, from the other side of the room.

"Please don't tell them."

"I won't. You should." Sighing, he turned, but couldn't see her beyond the glow of her flashlight beam. "Did you know that Troy's oldest Navy buddy stopped speaking to him because of what we do? The studio won't even let Ben and Jasmine go on a normal date, much less show off her ring. Rachel's headaches are getting worse, no matter what she says, and we all know our best evidence will stay locked in the archives until someone decides the public is ready for it, so in the meantime the audience thinks we're either idiots or frauds. And me – I spend my days behind an alias online, and my nights being a total jerk on camera. This team already has too many secrets, Dylan."

He was halfway down the hall by the time he heard her follow.

On the ground floor, despite their claims of fatigue, the others chattered happily about footsteps and faint voices and knocking and shadows where none should be. No one seemed to notice that Paolo and Dylan didn't contribute. The single duffel bag of equipment took mere minutes to re-pack, and then they were all back in the van, the headlights whitening the lane ahead.

"So what about the attic, you two?" Troy asked, as the talk began to die down. "Anything else exciting happen?"

Paolo looked toward Dylan. In the rear seats of the van, every team member was just a darker piece of the night. He could feel her gaze, but she didn't move or answer.

"Not a damned thing," Paolo said.

The others fell silent. It was a thoughtful silence.

Finally, Dylan sighed. "You are such an ass," she murmured. Despite her words and in the dark, Paolo could feel her reluctant, nervous smile.

"You get used to it," he said, and offered her a genuine one of his own, unseen.

Very Special Episode

"Not to tell tales on anyone," Rachel said, "but I think you should all know that when Ben first joined the team, Jasmine wasn't around yet, so he cast those longing eyes elsewhere…" She paused meaningfully.

Beside her, Ben turned a dull red as the room filled with catcalls and whistles.

"Be honest, Ben." She turned to face him and the rest of the head table. "As soon as you saw our storeroom full of gadgets, your heart was *ours*."

Ben put his face in his hands as the audience erupted again. Jasmine, shaking with laughter, slid an arm over his shoulders as if in comfort. He used the new closeness to steal a lingering kiss.

At the team table, Troy shared a fond look with Maddy and earned a kiss of his own. Beside Maddy, Mitchell beamed at everyone as if he'd baked them from scratch.

"I'm gonna vomit," Paolo muttered. Only Dylan heard him, since the seat on his other side was empty.

"Oh, for God's sake," Dylan whispered in exasperation. "Haven't you been to a wedding before? This is what it's like: embarrassing stories and bad jokes and yes, public affection. Shut up and be happy for them."

"Not that," Paolo said, hardly audible. "I need my phone."

"Well, too bad. Collecting them all at the door was a great idea. No one can put anything online, and it gives Rachel a rest from Wi-Fi."

147

"Yeah, yeah." He turned distracted eyes to Rachel. Dylan noticed his linen napkin had been twisted so tightly it hadn't started to unwind yet.

Troy looked over with a frown, and she shrugged slightly at him. He seemed to assess Paolo's condition with a glance, then moved his chin in a motion that was familiar team code for *Take care of it.*

Dylan suppressed a sigh and whispered again to Paolo. "It might be time for you to admit you have an addiction to technology." She kept her tone light but eyed the fist wrapped around his water glass. "And you're going to break that." He released his grip and shot her a scowl she rated about 5.5 out of 10 on the DeSanto scale: not aimed at her so much as the situation. After more than a year of working with him, she knew it well.

Eventually he said, with an angry reluctance, "It's not – it's – my phone gives me something to focus on besides the crowds." He glared sideways at the room full of party guests and his glass-less fingers started drumming on the table.

"Hey." Before she could think about it, Dylan slapped her hand over his. "You've survived worse at conventions, where you're the centre of attention. This you can handle. Take a breath."

Rachel had said something else funny – the room was laughing – but Dylan missed it. Paolo had shifted his gaze from their hands to her face, and she lost a moment trying to read his expression.

What is it you're doing? her spirit asked with interest.

I have no idea, she thought, as Paolo's attention moved back to Rachel. His hand remained stationary under Dylan's, and although she tried to tune in to the speech again, she now felt conspicuous and awkward. If anyone looks over, she thought, it'll seem like I'm holding hands with Paolo, for God's sake.

You are, the spirit said. *And his energy is settling. It's almost like you're holding him in place,* it added thoughtfully. *Tethering him.*

"Shut up," she muttered.

One of Paolo's knuckles moved beneath her palm. "Are you talking to Connie, or me?" he asked in a low voice.

A familiar irritation washed through her embarrassment. She pulled her hand away. "Its name is not Connie," she said.

"Well, you can't keep calling it 'it,'" he said. "You have to call it something."

"Connie's a girl's name. It's not a girl."

"Could be short for Connor. Or Conway."

"It's not a boy, either." All of this was familiar ground, though the names themselves were new. They always were. Dammit, she'd fallen back into the months-long conversation before she'd even realized it.

"So just call it Con. Salute to its origin, right?"

Rachel's voice echoed more dramatically from the head table. "A toast," she said, raising her champagne flute. "To the bride and groom. Congratulations, felicitations, *mazel tov* and every other good wish."

Everyone at the team table raised their glasses and offered congratulations with the rest of the audience. Dylan smiled as Ben and Jasmine, radiant and laughing, lifted their glasses in return. The guests whistled and applauded as the couple shared another kiss, and Rachel handed the microphone to Ben. Jasmine crowded close but kept both hands free to sign as he put an arm around her shoulders.

"Uh, I won't talk long," Ben said hesitantly. "It's not one of my strengths. But I don't see any gadgets to fix, and they tell me this is kind of a tradition, so…" He shrugged, which earned him a gentle chuckle from the listeners. "I did want to thank you all for coming. And, um. I'm going to let Jasmine do the rest, because she's better with words than I am." He turned to face her, and his face brightened as she signed. "We are both so glad to have you here, and so blessed to have you all in our lives. We have to give special thanks to our families, who have been so supportive: we love you all." He and Jasmine joined the round of applause that went up. "And another thanks to our colleagues, without whom we would never have met. Guys, you're the best secret keepers in the world, and you make work fun." The newlyweds turned to face the *OpHaunt* table, and the eyes of the room turned with them.

As Troy and Mitchell waved cheerfully, Dylan felt Paolo stiffen in his chair and heard his faint intake of breath. Without thinking she moved, clasping his nearest hand and yanking it out of sight beneath the table to hold tight. Smiling widely, she used her other hand to raise her glass in acknowledgement, hoping she looked natural.

"We love you in a different way," Ben added, apparently on his own initiative. Jasmine grinned and blew them a kiss as the guests laughed again. Gradually, everyone's attention turned back to the head table. "So... I guess that's about it."

He handed the mic back to Rachel, who immediately turned to the audience. "Speeches over – this is the fun part! Go enjoy yourselves."

The sound system flared into life, and in an instant people were milling everywhere, as if they'd stepped out of the walls. While the room around them became a circus of noise and activity, Paolo's hand clutched Dylan's. From the head table, Rachel looked their way, and the satisfied curl of her smile prompted Troy to look over as well.

Rachel knows what you're doing, Dylan's spirit said.

"She always knows," Dylan muttered.

"I'm out," Paolo said, pulling his hand from hers. He stood so fast the glasses on the table were still swaying as he disappeared through the doorway behind them, out onto the verandah.

Troy nodded once at Dylan in the team shorthand for *good work.*

Maddy leaned in, calling to Dylan over the centrepiece. "How did you get him to stay so long?"

You tethered him, her spirit said proudly.

"I'm not sure," Dylan said.

"Whatever it was, we might have to put it in your job description," Troy shouted over the din as he pulled Maddy onto the dance floor.

Rachel made her way to the table and collapsed with a sigh into Paolo's chair. "Thank God that's over."

"You did a great job."

"Aw, thanks. But now the pressure's off and I can enjoy myself. I mean, they're all very nice and some of them are pretty fun, but I feel like I've been helping with this wedding for months."

"You have been."

"Years, then."

Oh. She's here – I'll go, the spirit told Dylan. *And something over there looks...* The voice drifted away as the presence did.

Dylan sent out a belated mental thanks, but the spirit didn't reply. She was relieved it had remembered to leave Rachel some space: they'd been working on that for months, too. The party should make things easier, since the spirit found crowds of people endlessly distracting. So it might be gone a while... or it might be back in fifteen seconds. Not for the first time, Dylan wished they could work out some sort of definite schedule between them, but the spirit didn't always seem to have the attention span or memory required.

In its absence, Rachel's shoulders relaxed and her smile widened. "Thanks, Connie," she called. Half the table away, Mitchell looked politely confused, but the noise of the room was such that no one else noticed.

Dylan kept her voice low anyway. "You and Paolo need to stop trying to name it."

"Why, did he suggest something?" Rachel blinked innocently. "Come on. You can't keep saying 'it'. That's just rude."

"It doesn't seem to mind."

"Hard to believe you don't get any sense of identity from it at all." When Dylan shrugged, Rachel pressed on. "It doesn't remember *anything* about its life? Family? Historical events. Fashion. Nothing?"

"I ask once in a while, but it gets kind of agitated, so I don't push. I don't think all that matters."

"Poor thing. We should try to find it some answers. Maybe if Paolo and Ben –"

"No way. Poor Ben hasn't even left for his honeymoon yet; I'm not handing him a to-do list for when he gets back. And Paolo has enough on his plate. Besides, come on, this is a party! Can we please not talk about work?"

"We could talk about your love life. Would that be appropriate wedding conversation?"

"In a depressingly ironic way, sure," Dylan said.

Rachel rolled her eyes. "Honestly, you two. What's it going to take?" Before Dylan could decipher this, Rachel leaned across the table toward Mitchell. "Mitchell! If you just sit there nursing that glass of wine you'll miss the best part of a wedding reception. Do you know what that is?"

Politely confused again, he shook his head at her.

"Members of the wedding party, hoping to make a new friend. You see that crowd of lavender at the bar? Those are our lovely, lovely bridesmaids – let's go see what we can find, shall we?" Cheerfully dragging the protesting Mitchell up out of his chair, she glanced back at Dylan. "Go dance, newbie. I'll find you. Unless someone else does first." She raised her eyebrows meaningfully and hauled Mitchell into the chaos.

Dylan, Dylan. She felt a familiar icy trail across her shoulders. *I wish you could see everything,* the spirit said, its voice whirling around her. *It's jumping bright like firecrackers over there… Why did you let Paolo go outside, when it's so much more interesting in here? Although his light does look better.* Now the voice came from between her and the verandah. *Quieter.*

"Good for him. That means I am off the babysitting clock and not worrying about it." She headed for the dance floor, and the spirit darted away, laughing to itself.

It was only much later – after the buffet was a ruin and the bar was closed and the DJ had hauled his gear away and the gifts were crammed into some parent's car and Jasmine and Ben were driving off, waving good-bye – that Dylan went back into the nearly-deserted hall and realized the spirit was still gone.

By ten-twenty the next morning, she couldn't wait any longer. She knocked on Rachel's door, churning with anxiety about the missing spirit and the dread of waking Rachel. The team knew from experience that Rachel and mornings weren't exactly –

The door opened, and a robe-clad Rachel blinked at her. "Dylan. Hey. Want some coffee?"

This was a good sign. "If you're having some."

"Silly question." She wandered back into the suite. "It's just about ready."

When Dylan reached the little kitchenette, Rachel was already filling a mug. Wondering how to begin, Dylan went to sit down but noticed the bundle of lavender satin just in time.

"Um, Rache?" She held up the camisole by its strap. "In case you were looking for this later."

"Ah." She plucked it from Dylan's hand and headed for the bedroom. "Very generous of you to think that would fit me, but thanks." She opened the door and tossed the camisole inside. The sounds of a running shower reached Dylan's ears before Rachel shut the door again.

"Sorry," Dylan said. "I can come back later if I'm interrupting."

"You'd still be out in the hall if you were. What's up?"

All Dylan's anxiety flooded back. "The spirit. It's gone."

"Gone?" Rachel stared at her for a moment. "Huh. I guess that explains the headache I don't have."

"It left last night during the reception and I haven't heard or felt it since. No voice, no cold spots, nothing. So this morning I went back to the reception hall – it was closed, but I walked all around it, calling. It's not there, either."

"It's never left you for this long before?"

"No."

Rachel frowned. "Not even overnight? Not in the – what? – year and a bit since it arrived?"

"No," Dylan said. "Never. And as far as I can tell, now it's been gone for almost sixteen hours."

Rachel considered her again. "Dylan," she said slowly. "How have you lived like that?"

"What? Like what?"

"If it's always around, when do you get a break?" When Dylan just blinked in surprise, Rachel went on. "I mean, from what you've said, all day it's asking questions and making comments, wandering off and reappearing without warning. How do you focus? And what does it do when you're asleep, if it doesn't leave? How do you know it's still there? Does it… is it in your dreams?"

"That isn't – I don't –" Uncomfortable, Dylan waved a hand. "That's not the issue here. The point is, it's gone. So how do we find it?"

"You're right: the point is, it's gone." Rachel leaned against the counter. "Maybe you should embrace that while it lasts."

"What? No, we have to figure out what's going on!"

"We aren't on a job," Rachel went on reasonably. "You don't need it to navigate some haunted place or scare away the boogies or tell you what's going on. But you also don't need it to be loitering nearby all day. It'll probably just come back on its own. Meanwhile, go do something and be genuinely alone. It's not a terrible thing."

"Excuse me?"

"Come on, Dylan," Rachel sighed. "You know my family history. You think I haven't seen people lose themselves when they let spirits get too close? Believe me, separation is healthy. Enjoy it."

Dylan was startled to realize how much her panic was rising as Rachel spoke. "So you don't care that it's gone?"

"That's not what I said."

"You don't see that I'm concerned for what might have happened?"

"I see you more than concerned," Rachel said. "I see you freaking out, which worries me."

"I came to you for help," Dylan said, unable to keep the accusation from her voice. She slid off her stool.

"I am helping." Rachel's voice was sharp enough to stop Dylan in mid-stride. "I'm trying to calm you down, just like I would any panicked client." Seeing Dylan was listening, she softened her tone. "Look, I do understand. And given how much it has become part of your daily life, of course you feel its absence. But as much as it may act like one some-times, it's not a child. It's not lost in the woods or trapped down a well. We never really know why spirits do what they do. So I think either it'll come back on its own, or else it's just… gone."

Mouth dry, Dylan just stared at her. Rachel at least looked apologetic as she shrugged.

"But… what should I do?"

"Like I said, enjoy this break. Beyond that, if you really want to find it somehow?" She frowned into her coffee. "No idea."

That shook Dylan almost more than anything else. Rachel always knew what to do.

"Okay," Dylan managed at last. She heard movement from the bedroom and realized she was in no mood to attempt a normal conversation with someone she didn't know. "I'll let you get back to your morning."

"Dylan –"

"No, I'm fine. It's fine. We'll talk later." She escaped before Rachel could say anything else.

The hotel's broad hallway was too bright, and the carpet pattern made her eyes water. Dylan wandered up and down it for a while anyway. She found Troy's door and was standing in front of it, fist raised to knock, when she remembered him and Maddy saying they were taking Nate to the theme park today. She circled the hallway a few more times.

Jasmine and Ben were on their honeymoon. Rachel didn't know what to do.

Which only left…

"Dylan?" Paolo's voice sounded unsure.

She turned and there he was, laptop in hand and room key dangling, frowning at her.

"Why are you just standing there?" He took a closer look at her face and his frown deepened. "What's wrong?"

"Depends who you ask." She tried a laugh, but it sounded pathetic even to her ears. "My – the spirit. It's gone. I can't find it, and I don't know what happened to it. It's never been away this long, I don't know if it's coming back. And I don't even know why I'm so…" Antsy? Worried? Lost? Each word made her squirm.

A door down the hall burst open for a chattering family, kids shouting about water slides.

"Okay," Paolo said quickly, and stepped in front of her. "Let's figure this out." He unlocked the door.

Her random stop in the hallway had been in front of his room.

This day just kept getting weirder.

⟨Ⴕ⟩

Dylan jerked awake when her phone rang, and fumbled across her bedside table until she found it. She squinted into the glare of the screen and groaned. Then she dropped it on the mattress, tapped the speakerphone on, and buried her face in the crook of her elbow.

"I'm going to set up your own ringtone," she mumbled, "so I can ignore you. It's three in the morning."

"So it is," Paolo said, "but I thought of something." He paused. "Is the spirit back yet?"

Dylan went still and silent, calling out in her mind, listening for any sound. Nothing. She sighed, digging the heels of her palms in her eyes. "No."

"Damn," he said. "Okay, listen –"

"It's been four days," Dylan went on tiredly. "Maybe it's just not coming back. Maybe it found someone else to hang around. I mean, we don't even know why it chose me in the first place. Or maybe it finally crossed to the other side or whatever. Good for it."

A dismissive noise bristled through the phone line. "You don't seriously think any of that. Have you been talking with Rachel again?"

"She came over to check on me. She brought pizza."

"Probably because she feels like shit for not helping you properly in the first place."

"She helped. She's been helping," Dylan said defensively.

His derision sounded again. "Belatedly."

The truth, Dylan admitted, was that Paolo had started it all, and Rachel and Troy had caught up as he'd railroaded past them. He'd started by bringing Dylan and a backpack full of sensors out to the reception hall when it opened for the day, questioning the staff and half-bullying them into allowing an impromptu investigation.

When nothing had turned up on the instruments, Dylan had suddenly thought of the DJ and all the electronics that might've drawn the spirit away. So Paolo had called Rachel and asked for the name of the service that had worked the reception. She'd said she didn't know it. "Ask that bridesmaid you left with," he'd suggested. Rachel had hung up on him but texted an hour later with a name.

DJ Travis had been a dead-end the next day – his equipment hadn't been giving him any trouble and he'd seemed increasingly bewildered by their questions about disembodied voices and cold spots. Dylan had taken pity on him, dragging Paolo and his 7.8 DeSanto scowl out of the office.

Rachel must've called Troy, because he'd stopped by to hear the full story, then had called Ben's parents to ask a series of seemingly innocuous questions about how everyone was feeling after the big day. Rachel did the same to Jasmine's parents, discovering that Ben and Jasmine had checked in only once, when their plane had landed – *everything was fine, they had a wonderful flight, champagne and everything, so nice of you all to send them first class* – and given the remoteness of the island, the newlyweds weren't expected to call again until they came home.

On day three, the remainder of the team had convened in Dylan's cramped living room and debated the likelihood that the spirit had returned to the site of the jail, even though the building itself had been demolished. Paolo had thought it might: that in a moment of crisis, it would be drawn back to the site's residual energies. Dylan had said she wasn't sure it had been in crisis when it left, or ever since.

"It's been separated from you, after more than a year," Paolo had said. "That's crisis."

Then Rachel had pointed out they didn't even know for sure that the spirit had been a prisoner in the jail – maybe it was an ancient spirit, or even an elemental, tied to a deep well or the very bedrock, which would mean it had been on the site for centuries before the jail was even built.

"Then it would definitely go back, building or not," Paolo had said, looking to Dylan for an opinion. "Road trip?"

That was when Dylan had realized – really realized – how little she knew about the spirit. Together every day for more than a year, and she couldn't even answer basic questions. What had she been doing, all that time?

Troy had noticed her rising distress, and to distract her, asked for a recap of what the spirit had last said at the reception. She'd skipped the part about tethering Paolo but repeated everything else.

"Something in the room was attracting it," Paolo had said.

"That doesn't narrow it down," Dylan had sighed. "It's always so curious about people, loves the energies generated by a crowd. A wedding reception must've been like Disneyland on a sugar high. Plus it had the light show, the music… it could've been anything."

The discussion had broken up soon after. Rachel coming back later with pizza hadn't helped much.

Now, half-asleep in her darkened room at three in the morning, Dylan heard Paolo say, "The presents."

"What presence?"

"The wedding presents, the gifts," he said impatiently. "The site itself is clean. The DJ checks out. We can't account for every guest, so for the sake of moving forward, let's assume that it's none of them. The only other things that would've left that room with no residual trace are the gifts."

Dylan moved her hands off her eyes and stared through the darkness at the ceiling. "The gifts," she said slowly.

"What?" Paolo said after a moment. "What are you thinking of?"

"It said 'something *over there*' and 'firecrackers *over there*'. I'm trying to remember if there was any… direction in its voice." He waited silently on his end of the line until she growled in frustration. "No. Maybe. I can't be sure."

"You don't have to be," he said. "We'll check them out tomorrow. Well, later today. Turns out all the gifts went to Jas and Ben's apartment, and Rachel has their spare key."

"How do you know all this?"

"Archivist."

"Yeah, right," she said. "More like, you've been waking up other people before you woke me."

"Meh," he said, and she could picture his shrug. "I'm not sure Rachel was technically asleep. Bridesmaid again."

"Oh, God," Dylan said, trying not to laugh. "Oh, poor Rachel. She is going to hate you so hard."

"Whatever," he sounded amused. "Everyone hates me."

"I don't," Dylan said.

There was a long silence.

"Get some sleep," Paolo said. "We'll pick you up around ten."

"Get some sleep yourself. I mean it."

The line went quiet again. "Sure." He hung up.

Later, he seemed as disappointed as Dylan when the pile of gifts checked out clear. Not so much as a bleep registered on any of their sensors. She couldn't place his scowl on her usual scale, though: part of it was about the situation but part of it was about her, somehow…

"We'll think of something else," he promised.

But they didn't.

⑪

"Back-to-work treats," Rachel announced as she swept into the conference room. "Aw, look at you two, already labouring away on your side-by-side laptops." She set a bakery box and a tray of take-out coffees on the table.

Paolo looked at the clock in surprise. "You're here early."

"First day back, client this afternoon, Jas and Ben still away. Lots to do." She started shrugging off her coat. "Help yourself. Is Troy in?"

"Thanks," Dylan said, reaching for a pastry. "Yeah, he's in the back office."

"Did you have a nice time with the bridesmaid last night?" Paolo asked, in what he thought was his innocent voice.

Wincing, Dylan shook her head.

"You know what, I did." Rachel tossed her coat on a chair and handed Paolo a coffee, leaning close with a bright smile. "Her name is Lisa, and you should learn it, sunshine, because that's how polite people talk. And because," she added, "I think you might be seeing her around for a while." She took two coffees and left the room, calling for Troy.

Dylan and Paolo exchanged a startled look. "Was she blushing?" Dylan asked.

"I think so. Never seen that before."

They stared at the doorway a while, then Paolo's computer screen caught her attention. "What are you working on? Wait – is that the Yorkside Jail?"

He let out a resigned sigh. "Yes, but you weren't supposed to see it yet. I'm just going through the old case and the records I collected, looking for anything useful I might've forgotten."

"Paolo. It's been more than a week. I think the spirit is just… gone. I hate to see you wasting your time."

"I'm not. It's work-related research. If Troy gives me a new case, I'll put it away." His expression was even less convincingly innocent this time.

They both looked up at the sound of the front door chime.

"Hello?" a familiar voice called. "Doesn't anyone work the front desk around here?"

"What the –?" Paolo muttered as he and Dylan hurried out to the front room. Ben and Jasmine were standing in front of the door, weary-looking but tanned and grinning.

"Why are you here?" Dylan asked, rushing over to hug them both. "You've still got a week away!"

Would you believe we missed you all too much? Jasmine signed.

"No," Paolo said.

"Yeah, even I don't buy that," Dylan agreed. "What's going on?"

"Hey, what are you two doing here?" Troy's pleased voice came from the hallway, getting closer. "Lose your calendar or something?"

"This warm welcome we're getting." Ben shook his head. "It's like we brought the tropics with us."

"Is that who I think it is?" Rachel was right behind Troy. "Because it couldn't possi –" Clutching her head, she staggered, slamming hard into the wall.

"Rachel?" Troy lunged to catch her as her knees gave out. "Rachel!" She sagged against his arm.

Everyone else was racing over when a familiar, distant voice sounded in Dylan's head.

Dylan? Is that you? Am I back?

She stopped short. "Is that you?" she whispered. Only Paolo heard her, looking up in disbelief. Then they both turned to Rachel in horror.

"Get back, get away from her!" Dylan cried. "You're hurting her!"

Everyone but Paolo stared at Dylan in confusion. Rachel murmured incoherently.

That's not me, the spirit said, sounding hurt and distracted. *Or it's not only me. This one is strong – almost too strong to hold now, with everyone here.*

"What are you talking about?" Dylan asked. The spirit's voice was fainter than she remembered, just on the edge of hearing. Paolo was snarling at everyone to shut up.

Ben, the spirit whispered. *He has to leave.*

Dylan's eyes snapped up to meet Ben's, who looked chagrined and moved quickly toward the front door. "I'm sorry. I'll be outside," he said. "I'll just – I'll keep going until she gets better. Text me." The door chimed as he left, and it echoed in the shocked silence.

"Are you there?" Dylan whispered. Nothing answered.

Rachel started to stir.

Troy kept an arm around her but glared at Dylan. "Explain. Now."

Jasmine whistled sharply to get everyone's attention. *It's why we're back so early,* she signed, looking shaken. *It just took some time to figure it out. Dylan's spirit hitched a ride on our honeymoon.*

Paolo found his voice before Dylan did. "How? Why?"

We didn't know at first. When we finally figured out what it was, we thought maybe it was just confused. Jasmine glanced at Dylan. *You've told us it doesn't have much of an attention span. But eventually we realized it was protecting something – or I guess, protecting us from something.*

"What the good goddamn was that?" Rachel muttered, pulling herself from Troy to slump against the wall. "Felt like my skull blew up. Like Dylan's spirit, but times a thousand and seriously pissed off." She raised her glazed eyes to blink at Jasmine. "Were you talking? I missed it."

"Jas says it was the spirit," Dylan said, "but it's something else, too."

Jasmine nodded worriedly. *It's attached to an heirloom Ben's uncle gave him before the wedding, as the "something old" part of that rhyme, you know? It's a gold belt buckle now, but made out of some sort of antique artifact his family melted down into smaller pieces to carry more easily when they fled the pogroms. Most of it was used for money during their escape, or lost in the meantime. The buckle's pretty much all that's left. Anyway, something else survived with it, and that thing is **strong**.* She signed the last word with extra emphasis. *At one point we convinced Dylan's spirit to let it go so we could talk to it, and it just about wrecked the place. Sliced Ben's arm with a broken glass.*

"Is he all right?" Troy asked. "Are you?"

She managed a smile and nod but didn't seem to notice that one of her hands had drifted to her scars.

"And the spirit – my spirit – is keeping it contained somehow?" Dylan asked. "I didn't know it could do something like that."

Apparently it can, Jasmine signed. *Your spirit says there's no reason in this thing, just... rage.* She swallowed hard. *It kept messing up our phones if we tried to call, and everything else we tried didn't work. Ben didn't want to just dump it in the ocean, so eventually we decided we needed help more than we needed beach time.*

"We're on it," Troy said firmly.

"You'll need Ben," Rachel said hoarsely. "He's got the artifact and the connection." She pushed herself up the wall, and the last dregs of colour slid from her face. "But I can't stay if he's – if that thing's here. Sorry."

"Don't be sorry," Troy said. "Be safe. Go take care of yourself."

"I'll cancel the client," Paolo said, moving toward the phone. It rang as he reached it.

Rachel held out her hand, her eyes still squeezed shut. "It's my dad. We might need his help."

Paolo frowned at her as he answered the call. "*Oper* – Yes. No, sir," Paolo said. "She's right here." He handed the phone to Rachel.

As she croaked "Papa, I'm okay," into the receiver, Troy shooed everyone else out the front door.

They stood in the parking lot, staring at each other.

"Hey," Ben called from the far corner of the lot. "Is Rachel all right? What'd I miss?"

☂

Dylan staggered into the conference room and collapsed into a chair. The mid-afternoon light was gold through the windows and she felt like she could sleep for a week.

I'm sorry I left you.

"Don't apologize," Dylan murmured, slumping backwards to stretch her legs under the table. "I'm just glad you were there for Ben and Jasmine. And you were a huge help today. We couldn't have done it without you."

I got distracted during the party, the spirit confessed. It seemed to be circling the room; every once in a while, an icy breeze would stir Dylan's hair, but in the next moment the voice would come from the far corner. If anything it seemed stronger than it had been when it first arrived, despite all that had happened since.

There was just so much, the spirit continued. *I think I remember coming to you once in a while, but you were... you were so loud and bright. I could hardly come close enough for you to hear me. And when Ben and Jasmine left, they were exploding, they were pulling everything out of the room with them: happy, sad, impatient, thankful, scared… A matching pair! It was the most amazing thing.*

"How could you resist?" Dylan smiled a little.

"Dylan?" Paolo came in with two glasses of water and set one in front of her. "Took a chance that maybe your throat was as sore as mine."

Seeing it, she realized how parched she was. "Lifesaver."

Oh, look…

With a curse, Paolo startled away from something Dylan couldn't see. She chuckled, and he looked around. "Oh. Right," he said. "I didn't know you two were…" He edged toward the door.

"Stay," she said. "It'll save me having to tell you everything later." She savoured her water as he pulled out a chair. "Although if I did, I would call at three a.m., just so you know how it feels."

"I'd answer." A very familiar crooked smile. "It's not like you'd be waking me."

"You haven't missed much. So you got swept out with Ben and Jasmine when they left…" she prompted the spirit.

"Wait," Paolo said. "Let me…" He darted from the room.

Just see that, her spirit marvelled. *I hardly recognized him in all that. How long have I been away?* It sounded suddenly unsure. *It is him, isn't it?*

"Of course it is."

Of course it is. Now it sounded amused.

Paolo returned with one of the radios they used on their investigations.

Oh yes, the spirit said happily. *Ben's new trick. This is fun. I can almost taste it when I do this, you know… It tickles.*

"Can't believe no one thought of this sooner," Paolo muttered, and twisted the dial into the fuzz of white noise.

"Hello? How's this?" A sibilant voice slid between the static. "Can you hear me?"

Dylan stifled a shudder. "We can hear you." It's creepy and unnatural, she thought, fervently hoping the spirit wasn't listening to her thoughts, but we can hear you.

"So you were with Ben and Jasmine," Paolo prompted. Dylan was glad to see he didn't look any more comfortable with the radio voice than she did. "This is after the reception?"

"Yes…We went to that place where everyone appears when others disappear. And I saw that the party was nothing compared to this. This was…" A hissing sigh was almost indistinguishable from the white noise. "It was everything, everywhere."

Paolo looked confused.

"The airport," Dylan said.

"That's the one," the voice said. "Overwhelming. I lost them – I may have lost myself." The static roiled, louder for an instant. "I don't remember, but then there was a sort of bloom of new energy, like a star, and I found them again because they were right next to it."

"That was the spirit in the belt buckle?" Dylan asked. "How could it be new? Jasmine said the thing was ages old."

"I don't know," the spirit said vaguely, "on the way to the airport it had been just a little whisper in a box they were carrying with them, and then suddenly it was screaming bright. Oh, no, I remember – they'd crossed that door that isn't a door, just before you go to where you leave. That gave me a push, too, when I followed them."

Dylan and Paolo stared at the radio, then at each other.

"Every day, all day with this, for more than a year?" Paolo muttered. "How are you still sane?" He twitched in his seat. "Hey!"

"Be nice." The static flared and hissed again. "I can change your colour. Just because I'm talking over tickles doesn't mean I can't reach you."

Paolo turned his incredulous expression toward Dylan, who'd figured something out in the meantime.

"The x-ray machine," she said. "Security check at the airport. Spirits feed on energy, right? Wonder what kind of treat an x-ray is."

"It was screaming bright," the rustling voice repeated absently, "but the x-ray push helped me fold around it." White noise filled the air awhile, then the spirit spoke again. "It dimmed down to weaker in the… plane? Because you get pulled apart, floating up. It's harder to stay and remember."

"Air pressure change," Paolo muttered. "I've wondered about that."

"But then we were on the ground again," the spirit went on. "In a new place. There were so many people, energies everywhere like I'd never seen, chaos again but smaller, swirling and catching. I could feel the spirit growing again. So I grew myself and tried, Dylan – tried to keep it from getting to our friends."

"You did an amazing job," Dylan said softly.

"And again today," Paolo added. "Thanks."

Dylan's eyes met his and saw he was remembering what she was: Ben, his face set and arms corded as he held down the iron-lined box they'd put the buckle in, trying keep it steady while Jasmine poured salt-water steadily into it, scooped with her other hand and poured again. Dylan and Paolo, holding lit candles in place on the table and just barely keeping up with Troy as he thundered again and again through the banishment. Rachel and her father on two different speakerphones, bellowing in a language Dylan didn't know but whose words wove between Troy's as if they'd been made to fit. Something in the room snarling and snapping from all the corners, rattling the heavy box nearly out of Ben's grip, flinging hot candle wax onto exposed skin and clawing at Troy's cheek until he bled.

Through it all, her spirit had been there, Dylan knew. She could feel it moving around the room as an occasional reassuring touch of frost or an urgent whisper about what to do next. Eventually, it had hissed through the channels of Ben's radio to report the malevolence was weakening, and the team had doubled their efforts.

It's over, her spirit had finally whispered in her ear. It had taken a few minutes for Dylan to convince everyone. They'd all stood there, panting and disheveled, until the spirit had remembered the radio trick and spoken through the static again.

"Sorry, Ben." Its susurration was eerie but sincere. "It's just a buckle now."

Rachel had started giggling first, exhausted and hoarse through the phone line.

Remembering it all was nearly as exhausting as doing it. Dylan sighed and rose stiffly to lower the blinds against the sun.

"I'm just glad you're back," she said. "I was worried."

A pause, then a feathery coolness trailed across the back of her neck. *You were?*

Of course, she thought, and sensed the spirit's confusion. "Why wouldn't I be? I didn't know where you were."

But Dylan, the spirit said. *You don't worry about me. That isn't how this works.*

She laughed a little. "I can't help it."

You didn't know where I was, the spirit said thoughtfully. *So if I told you, you wouldn't worry?*

"Maybe."

I'm going to go explore. It paused. *Is that enough? I don't know all the place names.*

"Explore?" Dylan repeated. "What do you mean? When?"

Now? the spirit said. *I got that little push from the not-door, and there was a lot of energy here today. I think I feel... restless? Is that right? When you're scratchy and distracted?*

"A restless spirit," Dylan murmured, and laughed a little. Paolo was frowning at her. She shrugged back wearily. "So you're just... going to go?"

I think so. I forgot there's so much to see when I'm not with you.

That stung a little. The spirit seemed to sense it; she got another feathery touch on her cheek before its presence backed away.

The radio's white noise flared and hissed again. "I do like when we go to new places and meet others like me," the voice murmured. "Or not like me, but they're usually not boring. Maybe when I come back we can do that again. But, Dylan, you should've seen it today. You and our friends like that, all your colour music energies together..." It trailed off.

"Firecrackers?" Dylan suggested, smiling a little.

"No, better. Something complete, not sparks with space between. They'll be here when I'm not." The static crackled stronger for a moment. "Won't they?"

Paolo jumped again, slapping at his cheek. "Stop doing that."

"Yes, they will," the radio said with satisfaction. "I can see."

"So this is good-bye?" Dylan said.

That word sounds like forever. The voice took up its familiar place above her shoulder. She remembered the thermal image from the Yorkside Jail, when it had first wrapped around her like a cloak. *What word means I'll come back so we can explore together again?*

Dylan shrugged, and had the distinct sense the spirit was amused.

Maybe you'll remember it while I'm gone, it said. A touch of cold landed on her forehead. *Watch the thermal if you don't hear me first.*

She stood for a moment, waiting, but nothing else happened.

"It's gone, isn't it?" Paolo asked quietly.

"Yeah, I think so." She dropped back in her seat, then reached over and turned off the radio. The new silence was loud. "For now."

"Sorry."

She nodded, and they sat for a moment. "It's weird," she said suddenly. "I mean, I'm sad, but… I guess I'd already accepted it as gone, accepted being alone in my own head again after so long. Like Rachel said, it's not a bad thing."

"Just different."

"Yeah. I could probably get used to it."

Paolo offered his crooked smile again. "I could get you a book of obscure riddles, if you ever feel like you're especially missing it."

"Not sure I'll miss that part," she said, smiling herself. "But listen, I wanted to say thanks. For being there, and for everything you did. When it first disappeared, I wasn't much help. Actually, I think I was kind of a mess."

He shifted uncomfortably. "You were upset. Weren't thinking straight for a while. It happens."

"Yeah, but it was… bizarre. I could see myself freaking out about it, but it shouldn't have bothered me so much. That's not me. I couldn't explain it. Part of me was watching myself have this reaction and knew it was ridiculous, but no matter what I said to myself…"

"You couldn't stop it happening? Yeah. I get that." Paolo's smile twisted into the sardonic one their fans would recognize. "Welcome to the world of anxiety. Rationality is hard to come by." He dropped his gaze to the table and drew endless circles with a fingertip. "Gotta say, you handled it better than some. At least you didn't lash out or snap at people until you pushed them away."

They sat in silence for a while again.

"Okay, how about this?" Dylan said carefully, hoping she was right. "As part of my gratitude for you sticking with me through this weirdness – and yes, it's clear you don't want gratitude but too bad, you're getting it anyway – I will try to return the favour. I mean, I know you usually have your phone to distract you, but maybe we could have a plan B, in case that isn't helping enough, or if it isn't there."

His answer took a few moments to arrive. "Well. You could always hold my hand, like you did at the wedding." His tone was half-joking, but he was still staring fixedly at the table, index finger still circling, circling. "Because that… seemed to help."

She let a heartbeat pass, but before he could try to shrug it off or claim he was kidding, she reached out and covered his hand with hers. The circling stopped.

Taking a deep breath, Dylan laced her fingers between Paolo's. "Anytime," she said.

He looked up, startled hope lighting his face, so she kissed him.

Thanks

I wrote "The Con" as a stand-alone story years ago and would not have continued to explore the *OpHaunt* possibilities if it weren't for the encouragement of friends and family, so to them I owe a great debt and a loud thank you. Travis Sentell and Carol Cregg offered invaluable advice in the early drafts and enthusiastic support since then – here's to the next decades of writerly angst and friendship, you two. Dr. Dominik Endres provided much-needed assistance with Ben's story, and any physics-related errors elsewhere are entirely my own fault, as are any factual errors in Troy's shipboard life. (That's what happens when an Army brat decides to write a Navy chaplain.) The book in your hands wouldn't exist without the vision and labor of Maureen Whyte and Julie McNeill, and certainly not without my dear friend and editor, Bernadette Rule. Many thanks to you all. ~BDF

The best minds are the open ones.